The Meadow Whispers

Ted Bun

February 2023

The Meadow Whispers

Published by Edward Yeoman

11160 Caunes Minervois France

www.tvhost.co.uk

Copyright © 2022 Ted Bun

All rights reserved. No portion of this book may be reproduced in any form without permission from the publisher, except as permitted by British copyright law. For permissions contact:
ted.bun@sunnybuns.me.uk

Cover by Edward Yeoman
ISBN: 9798375634975

Imprint: Independently published

Dedication

Mrs Bun for her kindness and forbearance while I am hidden behind a computer screen and for her editing suggestions.

    And to

Linda Amstutz, for the snarky comments and suggestions that help make this book truer to its setting.

Contents

Chapter 1 1
Chapter 2 7
Chapter 3 15
Chapter 4 23
Chapter 5 37
Chapter 6 49
Chapter 7 55
Chapter 8 69
Chapter 9 81
Chapter 10 105
Chapter 11 109
Other Books by Ted Bun 117
About Ted Bun...119

Chapter 1

It was an early afternoon in July. I was driving out of town, the town of Oak Lees, South Carolina, population 1607, to be precise. I'd been visiting a witness in a fraud story I was working on. Oh yeah; I am a freelance investigative journalist cum PI, Marlon Gates. Perhaps you have read some of my stuff? I had a story about a Senator and his sister syndicated coast to coast.

I'd gotten what I needed and there was nothing to keep me in town, so I was leaving. I wanted to get a good way north before it got dark. There was little to stay for, I'd Googled Oak Lees before leaving home. It doesn't even have a Mac D's. The only thing that caught my eye was some place called Oak Leeves Camping Ground. It was rated by visitors at over four stars. "Wow, something that popular in a dead and alive place like Oak Lees!" I clicked the link to the website. Then quickly shut the window.

I was heading down Main Street, or what would once have been Main Street, before the automobile made weekly city shopping a reality. On the sidewalk, I saw something that made my blood boil. A bulky man kicking seven bells out of a dog.

Now you have to understand I love dogs, all dogs. As a kid, I had wanted a dog of my own but I was denied one. I suppose growing up in a Chicago tenement building, my parents made the right call. However, it means that I now love all dogs as any of them could have been mine.

I got out of my vehicle to remonstrate with the kicker. "Hey! You! Leave that dog alone!" I hollered, keeping well out of his reach. I don't like violence and always try to avoid it. Rather than getting bashed up like fictional detectives and journos, I subscribe to the running away is the best form of defence school.

The dog-kicker started getting abusive and came after me. I jumped back into the car and pressed the start button. The engine was already running and I have now accidentally turned it off. Before I had restarted the motor and got moving, he arrived and started pounding the hood with his fists. I could see he was causing a bit of damage to the bodywork. I had to do something.

I got out, keeping the bulk of the car between us; I shouted at him to stop. He moved forwards in an effort to get to me. I stepped sideways to keep the car … and I fell down the curb. In a flash, he was on me and aimed a kick at my body. I rolled away and sprang to my feet. You have to be fit to run away, so, I go to the gym a couple of times a week. My assailant swung a punch at me. I ducked and it missed. I threw a counter punch, a straight right into his chest, I'd put all my weight behind it. Yeah, it was a boxing gym, I had been coached some. He staggered back and fell, his head hitting the road.

Time to be somewhere else if I wanted to get back North, away from the heat and stifling humidity, by tonight. I drove away, the dog had run off so there was no reason to stay. I was on the outskirts of town when my police band scanner crackles to life. A scanner is a tool of my trade, the police tend to turn up at the scene of the most interesting stories.

"All cars, the Sheriff's brother has been assaulted and beaten up. The suspect was seen leaving the scene in a blue Dodge Charger." Shit! my car! "The perp is a white male, wearing chinos and a green and white striped shirt." Shit, Shit! My choice of gear for this trip. "The suspect is known to be violent, approach with extreme caution!" Shit, Shit, Shit! That meant 'stick him' first and keep on sticking him until he stops resisting. I'd heard that story many times, mainly, but not uniquely, from men of colour.

I needed to get away; I was certain that the dashcam would show the truth, that and the rear cam. It was a sophisticated system, but very useful for collecting evidence. If that footage could be delivered to an honest lawman... that wasn't going to happen in this town. Time to be somewhere else.

I drove away from town at the limit plus ten. Fast, but not that fast as to attract attention. It was all going well until a Black and White passed me heading in the opposite direction. I hit the gas hard even before the notification came over the radio.

"Sheriff, I just passed a blue Dodge heading out of town on County Road. I am turning and in pursuit."

"Roger that Carl, I am rolling County Road northbound. Any other units in a position to assist?"

"Sheriff. Denis, I'm on County Line, I can block County Road in about two minutes."

"Good job, Denis, Get the stinger deployed and wait. Carl, hold back I'll be with you about the time we hit County Line."

Trapped, even at ninety-five, I wasn't going to reach County Line before the road was blocked. The GPS suggest I had six miles to run. No turnings, no visible farm tracks ... except the one leading to Oak Leeves. If I could get there maybe the presence of witnesses might protect me a little bit. At least I wasn't being hotly pursued, I had a chance, a few minutes.

The GPS said I was four hundred yards short of the track to the campground entrance. I braked as hard as I could without locking the tires and leaving a huge clue on the road and turned gently into an orchard at the side of the road. The Dodge was hidden from easy view behind the trees.

I got out of my clothes, the main way of identifying me the Sheriff's Deputies had as if my life depended on it. I took almost all of the cash out of my wallet and transferred it to a money belt. I left a few bills in it to act as a decoy, enough to hint that I had misplaced my wallet. Having fished out most of the cash, I abandoned it in the passenger footwell. It still contained all of my cards and documents. They would be of no use to me in my current situation. The Sheriff's team would know exactly who I was as soon as they have the Dodge's registration.

Already tucked in the money belt, for emergencies like this, I have a set of alternative documents and some ID in another name. I have always found having a spare driver's licence and fake bank cards instantly available useful in both my lines of work. Finally, I recovered the camera's remote memory store from under the dash. As I said, it is a special dashcam set-up.

All packed, I put the money belt on bandolier style. I paused, listening for traffic. I heard one then another Black and White tear up the road. I listened for a few seconds more, then I legged it through the trees parallel to the road. The GPS had indicated that it was just a few hundred yards to the gates to Oak Leeves Naturist Resort.

Back in the last millennium, I had sold a story to a syndicate. To celebrate, I took my first wife on a long weekend camping break in Florida. Sounds cheap, well the story didn't fetch that much. Our accommodation was a mobile home, near a lake. I thought, swimming, canoeing, maybe a little hiking, in search of some outdoor 'adventure'. No chance. The first lizard induced screams and she never set foot outside the screened lanai for the whole stay.

I did learn about camping ground security. A barrier across the road and an old guy checking your registration plate to make sure you were registered. It would be easy to slip through.

Chapter 2

I arrived, panting hard, at the big gate to the resort. I hadn't even given a thought to the odds that a nudist campground would be so security aware. It was surrounded by a tall fence and solid-looking gates. As I searched the surroundings of the entrance, hoping to see a bellpush or something that would enable me to get the gate open, I saw someone coming out through a smaller pedestrian gate, I was in luck!

"Taking a big risk there, my friend" The man exiting the site laughed. "You know that the local Sheriff hates this place, don't you? He would bust you for lewd behaviour just for stepping out of the gate let alone going out for a jog dressed like that! Get in quick.!"

I was too busy trying to bring my breathing back under control to utter anything other than, "Thanks!" I was in, I was out of the reach of the Sheriff for a while, as long as these people were willing to protect me.

My breathing slowly steadied. I walked in the direction signposted to the Reception, Office and Maintenance. I found myself outside a single log cabin surrounded by a wide shady porch. I let myself in and was met at the counter by a naked woman.

OK, so I had seen a fair number of naked women in my time. Two of them had been my wives. This was the first one with grey hair and boobs that pointed towards the ground rather than at me. "I guess you want to check in, Sir. Would that be for a day visit, or do you plan a longer stay?" There was a burst of static from an old-fashioned radio behind her. She must have had a good idea who I was.

"Can I register for the day? And, if I can get settled, maybe a night or two?" I was feeling a little unsure of how to behave. I have never had a business conversation with a naked woman before, well not completely naked. And, unlike when I had negotiated with the stripper, I had been dressed throughout that stag night encounter.

"That'll be fifty bucks for the day. Plus, a Single Male Conduct deposit of another two hundred. You get that back if we don't have to throw you out." She smiled at me, "I expect you'll get it back; you don't look like a trouble-causer. I'll need some ID too." I counted out the cash and handed over my ID.

"Thank you, Mr Galpin. Unless that belt has more tricks than a monkey, you'll need to hire a towel and buy a bottle of sunscreen."

"Theo, please," I looked at the

nameplate on the desk. "Mary, how much for the towel and some factor twenty?"

"Factor fifty I think, Theo. Thirty dollars and I'll lend you a towel." She laughed and muttered something about 'Cottontails' as she selected a bottle from the display.

The radio squawked. I missed the words but they were angry. "If I were you, Theo, I'd go find the pool. The Sheriff will be here in a few minutes and I gather he is looking for someone."

I hurried in the direction Mary had pointed and draped the towel over an unoccupied sunbed, as the practice seemed to be. I was lying flat on my stomach, taking stock of the people around me when a Black and White rolled up along the road in the direction of the office. What I had taken in was that at fifty-two I was one of the younger people. I also had one of the slimmer bodies.

"I wonder what the Sheriff wants now?" The woman on a sunbed next to the pool stairs asked loudly of no one in particular. "Do you reckon he wants another eyeful of my hooters? I mean the way he was staring the last time."

"I ain't that certain it ain't ma nuts he is after stroking!" A head had appeared over the edge of the pool.

"What would he be wanting with your junk, Duane?"

"Do I have to remind you every time? It tain't junk, it all works perfectly, Joannie."

"Well, it sure is quick, I'll give you that!" Joannie started laughing.

"I dunno why I married you woman, I think the Sheriff has a higher regard for my attributes than you!"

"You married me because I'm the one that makes you so darn quick." Then she must have spotted me. "Hush my mouth now! I am embarrassing the young Cottontail here."

"Howdie! I'm Duane." He levered himself out of the pool. I had a quick glance, nothing special. Nothing I hadn't seen at the gym. "Potty-mouth on the sunbed, that's my wife, Joannie. You'll have to excuse her, she might have had a cocktail too many. And you are?"

"Theo Gal…"

"No surnames here, Theo, it is a privacy thing." The Sheriff's car drove off, accelerating hard. "As it appears, Mary has just reminded the Sheriff about that too." Duane finished as the Black and White shot down the paved track.

"Theo needs to get some sunscreen on or his bits are going to burn." Joannie pointed vaguely in the direction of my junk. "Duane, get on and spray his back."

Duane signalled that I should stand up and sprayed my factor fifty on my back. "You can rub it in for yourself and then the front is all down to you. Do it carefully or you'll regret it. You can take my word for it! The sun can be a bitch in these parts, or do I mean on them?" He chuckled at his own joke.

I got myself factored up. Doing my junk was a bit embarrassing and I got very self-conscious, so I was forced to lie face downwards. After a few minutes of people-watching, I was getting bored. I mean watching people sitting in groups of four, maybe eight, holding drinks and chatting isn't great entertainment, even if they are all naked.

"Mary has got a selection of books up in the office if you want to read something!" Joannie must have read the situation. I climbed off the sunbed and quickly wrapped the towel around my waist. I was in gym mode. "That's a giveaway too, throw your towel over your shoulder, like that!" She moved her head to direct my eyes towards a younger woman who was leaving the pool area. She had her towel hanging from her shoulder, across one of her breasts and down to her pubic region. I did a quick double take, she was shaved smooth. My second wife, or my first for that matter, didn't spend much time naked outside the bathroom. They may have trimmed, but I hadn't seen a clean-shaven woman, apart from accidental misdirections when doing online research, that is.

I got the hint though and arranged my

towel in a similar manner. Joannie gave me a thumbs up and I strode confidently towards the office. OK, so confidently might not be the right word but trepidatious sounds so much like a made-up word.

"Well, you missed all the excitement, Theo." Mary was still behind the desk when I reached the office. "I had the Sheriff in causing a ruckus again. Last month it was about leading some of the local youth astray! I mean us, leading schoolboys up a fifty-foot tree so that they could see over the fence! We said to him if the kids want to see so bad, their folks should ring and we'll book the family a tour, didn't we Greg?"

"He certainly didn't like it when I suggested we would counter-sue for invasion of privacy" A slim, grey-haired man appeared from a doorway behind the counter. "Hi, I'm Greg, you must be Theo. Nice to meet you, young man."

We shook hands, I instantly liked Greg. It had been a long time since anybody called me 'young man' so that was a good start. "Do you have a lot of trouble with the Sheriff then?"

"It would make an interesting story for that guy the Sheriff is after busting. I just looked him up on Google. Turns out he is some sort of a journalist, he has written a few interesting exposés. It might just be a story for him, mind he'd have to stop overnight. It is a very long story."

"Talking of which, it happens that I was going to ask Mary here if I could book to stay for one night, while I was picking a book to read."

"That, young Theo, could be a very good idea. I heard the Sheriff ordering his Deputies to be extra vigilant of movement in this area. Would you credit it? They have even staked out the suspect's vehicle against the event that he might come back to it!"

"You seem well informed, Greg." A snort from Mary suggested she was getting a little frustrated about the dancing around going on.

"The Sheriff turned up at the gate, claiming to be in pursuit of a wanted felon," Greg informed me. "He was 'in pursuit' so I had to let him in, or we would have faced charges of obstructing him in his lawful duty. He storms in here demanding we tell him where this Gates guy is."

"I say to him, that nobody by that name is in the resort. I even show the register. Nobody has checked in since you did, at twelve forty-five, Theo." Mary smiled.

I had been shortly after two when I had checked in. I knew it, she knew it but the register distinctly said twelve. They knew who I was all right. Mary had doctored the register.

"Besides, if someone had battered the Sheriff's Brother I expect they would be showing signs of having been in a fight; the odd bruise and cut knuckles. That thug wouldn't have gone down easily."

That was something Greg had gotten wrong, one proper punch, somewhere soft. Just one blow had put him down. It had gone exactly how the guys at the gym had said it would. "Heads are harder than fists, bare knuckles are for body blows." I was unmarked.

"So, I thought it couldn't have been you, besides the radio had described a bigger man, maybe one hundred and ninety pounds and six-two." I'd missed that bit, probably after I had dumped my car. "It would have taken a big man to best that slob!" Mary chuckled. "I have you down for cabin fourteen, I wondered when you'd come for the key."

"Shall I get your bags, Theo?" Greg was laughing as he walked back into the office. It wasn't until then I realized he was butt-naked too. Had I really stopped noticing?

"Don't forget you wanted a book." Mary reminded me, as she handed me the key to cabin fourteen.

Chapter 3

"Theo?" I was lost in my book. It was one of those space opera-type science fiction stories. The hero had been just about to jump into hyperspace when the tractor beam had fastened onto his spaceship. I almost jumped myself as the female voice intruded into my reality.

I rolled onto my side and looked up into an attractive, if slightly pensive, face. Blue eyes, high cheekbones, framed by loose-styled blonde hair. One thing for certain she wasn't my ex-wife. The coloring was one thing, that she was naked, in the open air, was pretty much the clincher. It was the woman with the draped towel from earlier. My eyes were sliding down her body, seeking confirmation, when I remembered that I was bare too. My eyes whipped back up to engage hers.

"Yes, I'm Theo, how can I help you? Miss?"

"It has been a while since I was a Miss, they call me Helen. Would you mind if I sat down?" She gestured to the sunbed next to mine. "I'd like a little chat with you." She dropped her towel onto the lounger and sat down before I had formulated a response.

"Sure thing, Helen, make yourself comfortable." This was a bold approach, an attractive woman, a naked woman, had just walked up to me and I wondered where this was going.

"I know who you are, I have been talking to Greg and Mary. I also do not doubt that you could discover that I am not Helen, very quickly. So, we have to take each other on trust." She stared into my eyes as if trying to read what lay behind them.

"Uhuh?" Well, what else could I say? Besides, I wanted to find out what this was all about and the best way to do that was to let Helen do the talking.

"I gather you have had a bit of a run-in with Sheriff Brown."

"I've never met the guy, Helen," I answered as truthfully as possible.

"OK, with the Sheriff's Brother, Emmet, then?"

"I might have done, why are you asking?"

"Maybe I just want to shake the hand of the man who put Emmet on the ground. Maybe I want to know what it is all about and maybe I'd like to know what the dashcam in the abandoned car had recorded."

"That's a lot of maybes. You seem to be remarkably well-informed."

"Yes, I have eyes and ears all over town. Including inside the Sheriff's Department. However, I am not prepared to discuss this in the open. I'd like you to join me for dinner tonight at the resort restaurant."

"What time?" I wasn't going to turn down a dinner invite from a good-looking woman. Then a thought hit me. "What about the dress code?"

She had gotten to her feet. "Seven? And come as you are, I gather you don't have much option!" She laughed for the first time and sashayed off. I decided that might just enjoy dinner.

I tried to settle back into my book, but the moment had passed. I decided to risk it all and I went for my first dip in the pool. I'd skinny-dipped in pools as a dare whilst a teenager. Always after dark, half-hidden in the shadows. Today I was going to have to walk to the pool in broad daylight. Then, I'd already survived several hours and got a naked date tonight, so I tried to walk tall, walk straight and look the world right in the eye, as the song goes.

As I walked, I felt my junk bouncing from side to side. It felt a bit sensual. I started to, well you know, I desperately hoped everybody else was looking me right in the eye! I ran the last few paces and dived headlong into the cool water. It was, yeah, it was …

It must have been half an hour later that I climbed out into the heat of the late afternoon sun. The water streamed down my body, cascading from my junk. Nope, that word had to go. I agreed with Duane, it was a rather belittling and derogatory thing to call it. Mine was all in working order, certainly the last time I used it. Working equipment, that was it, my equipment.

*****

There was a gentle buzz of conversation, indistinct over the background music, as I walked into Cheeks Restaurant, dressed in my best towel. I caught sight of Helen, talking to Greg near the servery. Greg waved and waited for me to join them. "I think I should do proper introductions. Theo, I'd like you to meet Helen, not her real name, one of the co-owners of this place. Helen, this is Theo, not his real name either, a guest that arrived just before the Sheriff this afternoon. Now, I'll leave you to talk." He pointed to a vacant table, tucked into a corner. "I'll come for your order in a few minutes."

"I'm guessing you don't go inviting all the single males to join you for dinner, Helen."

"So the profile Greg pulled off the internet is accurate, Theo, not his real name, freelance investigator and journalist. Age 52, married twice, currently single." She paused, "Currently single?"

"Yes, you have got me. I haven't had a point of access to do a reciprocal search, so a little about Helen would be nice."

"Helen, age 47, divorced, daughter of the financial backers of this resort amongst other interests." She was pretty and had a nice way about herself. I bit my tongue and refrained from asking about the ancient city of Troy, too obvious I decided.

We both ordered the steak and salad, I added a portion of fries; I hadn't eaten since breakfast. I was going to ask about wine, but then I realised I was dangerously low on cash, my fake cards were exactly that, fake. I was preparing to settle for water when Helen ordered, "a bottle of my usual, please." A bottle of Napa Valley Merlot arrived just before the food.

"That is a nice wine!" I had enjoyed my first sip.

"It should be, I have it shipped here specially." Helen sniffed the aroma of the wine, held it up to the light then took a breathy mouthful. "Then, it never lets me down."

"OK, can we cut to the chase, you wanted to talk to me." From the moment she had interrupted my chase across the galaxy, I'd wanted to talk to her too. That part of our conversation would have to wait though.

"My ears in town said that the man Sheriff Brown wants to resist arrest was heard shouting at Emmet Brown, but they didn't hear the words. My eyes then saw the same suspect land a single blow on Emmet, knocking him to the floor. The suspect then drove off."

"You are remarkably well-informed, Helen. Did your ears or eyes find out why I was in South Carolina and Oak Lees in particular, this morning?"

"Nope, I am not that well informed. Is it relevant?"

"Not really, I was just wondering how much of the town's business you know about."

"Not enough, that is why I need your help. What happened that got you involved with Sheriff Brown and his gang?"

I noted her use of the word 'gang' and related the tale of the dog kicker. "So, I decided that it was time to leave town. Then the radio went crazy."

"And your dashcam recorded all this?"

"How do you know about my dashcam?"

"Friends who work for the police. You know … sources." She smiled and tapped her nose, reminding me of the journalistic code. "My informant had access to your vehicle after the Deputies found it. He noticed that the memory card was missing. I have every reason to believe that you still have it."

"If I do, what happens next?"

"I'd like to see what you have recorded and if it is what we hope, I want to send a copy to a member of my family. We need to hide the original somewhere very safe. Greg and Mary cannot stop the Sheriff if he has a warrant to search the resort."

"What is in this for you? Why are you so keen to help me, Helen?"

"It is a long story, would you mind if we took it somewhere else? These chairs are not the most comfortable."

I didn't mind, after a couple of glasses of wine, I was relaxed about whatever Helen had planned. Although, "What happens if the Sheriff turns up with his search warrant?"

"He is unlikely to, Theo, he got a tip-off about a figure dressed in combat fatigues moving through the woods a few miles east of here." That solved that.

The Meadow Whispers

Chapter 4

We settled into comfortably cushioned cane chairs on the insect-screened balcony of what must have been the largest building in the resort. The moonless sky was filled with a myriad stars. The air was warm and we had the last glasses of Helen's delightful wine to hand.

"The story goes back many years, in fact before the War of Independence."

"You said it was a long story but if that is where it begins, we will need more wine." What was I saying? "Please, carry on, you have got me hooked." How strong was that wine? Shut up, Marlon. I shut.

"Back then the Carolinas had substantial French holdings dotted around the place. Most of them were ceded to the new America. Others were bought from their French owners. For some reason, the status of this patch of land wasn't legally settled until sometime in the late nineteen fifties. Which meant it wasn't included as part of the county when the county lines were drawn. That was an anomaly that the Brown family discovered and exploited.

They bought the place, dirt cheap. Who else wanted half-a-dozen acres of scruffy orchard miles from town? Then they built a Casino on the site. They avoided Federal and State legislation on gambling claiming that the casino was technically in France." She took a sip of wine. "Things ran along smoothly for many years, everybody accepting the post-war situation as de facto. Then things changed slightly, Grandpa Brown died and his sons got greedy. They added liquor sales and prostitution to the casino business. There was a suggestion of narcotics being moved across the state borders, the Feds became involved. They were the people who discovered that the national status of the land had changed years earlier."

"How had they missed it when it happened?" I was hooked on the story. Hooked, good and proper; stories like this were my bread and butter.

"Custom and practice. The existing pattern was well established, nobody was looking at it until the FBI took a detailed look.

"Pa Brown reacted quickly. The drug supply business moved on to a new location. He got rid of the overt prostitution. He turned the place into a casino hotel. It rented rooms. What went on in those rooms was a matter for the consenting adults renting it. He bought a Judge and got the liquor licence regularised. It cost a lot, Judges don't come cheap. So he took a different approach when taking control of law enforcement.

"He got his Son, Huck, elected as Sheriff, and Sheriff Brown was seen to take his duties very seriously. Regular inspections, visits and raids of the casino took place. A few fines for underage drinking were issued. A few tickets for drunk driving were handed out on the road outside. That was the first sign that things weren't right. Political opponents of Sheriff Brown got tickets his supporters didn't."

The wine glasses were empty, she went to fetch some more from the kitchen. "You might notice a slight difference in the flavour, this bottle has been breathing since last night." Helen leant across me to top up my glass. So close, I imagined I could feel the warmth of her skin almost brushing mine.

"So, where did it all go wrong for this slick operation?" All this background was interesting, but it didn't get me any closer to my clothes.

"The Gambling Commission raided, without support from the Sheriff's Department and found certain irregularities. I gather that they were planning prosecutions for a range of code violations. Then one night, the place caught fire. The town's Fire Trucks were all responding to a false alarm at a farm south of the town, by the time they arrived, it was too late."

"An insurance scam?" I had to ask, journalistic curiosity had kicked in.

"The insurers thought so, they turned the claim down flat. Then the bank foreclosed on a loan."

"A loan? I would have thought they would have been minting money!"

"I would have too. However, during the due diligence, before our syndicate bought the land, someone spoke to one of the bookkeepers from the casino. He revealed that the Browns had faced significant costs in remodelling the bordello into a hotel at a time of reduced cash flow. They had borrowed as much as the bank would lend."

"The failed insurance scam must have left them very short of the money to service the loan. Hardly any wonder the bank foreclosed."

"That and the fact that Pa Brown vanished. Rumours circulated of a deeper involvement with the mob. Stories of vehicles with New York plates arriving late at night and disappearing before dawn were common currency among the regulars at the casino. Of course, there was never any follow-up by the Sheriff."

"Interesting, but it is just speculation and no proof of any wrongdoing."

"That's true, sorry, Theo, I was getting sidetracked by the conspiracy theories."

I was getting to like the way Helen said, 'Theo.' I might not ever let her call me Marlon! There, I'm getting ahead of myself again. "The casino has gone, the land is held by the bank and the big boss has vanished. How do we get from there to where we are now?"

"That is … Look at the time, I'm going to fix some snacks. Can you give me a hand in the kitchen?"

I agree and follow her into the cabin. She fishes a couple of packs of frozen nibbles out of the freezer and scatters a few on a baking sheet. "Can you put these back for me, please?" She hands me the remaining snacks. I wait while she bends over to put the tray in the oven, and then I step around her when she stands up. There was a pause while she studied me intently.

"Can I trust you, Marlon?" She broke the silence.

"I'd prefer if you called me Theo, while I am here, please, Helen." I decided that I would like to have her call me Theo every day of the week.

She looked me straight in the eye. Holding my gaze as if she was trying to look into my soul, searching for signs of deception or deceit. After what seemed like an age she broke eye contact and moved across the kitchen. As reached up into a cupboard for a plate, her arm brushed against my shoulder.

After placing the plates on the counter next to me she repeated her question. "Can I trust you, Theo? I mean, really trust you?"

"I would like to think you could. The journalist and his sources — it is a long tradition."

"And if the source is the story?"

"Honesty, probably sympathetic honesty. Something like …" I was hunting for an example, one from my early days as a local paper stringer. "The mechanic who told me he had polished the distributor cap, topped up the lube and charged for a full service. After I had checked, the story became him being the whistle-blower on a widespread scam."

"I can see how you could have stitched him up." Helen bent forwards to check the snacks through the oven window. "I think they might be done, pass me the oven gloves."

I pass her the cloth mittens and she opened the door. The wave of hot air hits us both. Helen stepped back and slipped. I grabbed hold of her to stop her from falling. I paused for the shortest time, while she steadied herself, and then I let go. I didn't want to but … was I answering her last question?

"Thank you, I'll bring the plate. Can you top up our glasses, please?" Something in her voice suggested I had passed a test.

*****

"I had to be sure, I was right putting my trust in you. You aren't one of us, a naturist. You were only admitted to the resort based on Mary's sense that, "my enemy's enemy is my friend" as it applies to Sheriff Brown. Since then, you have tried to adapt to our ways and haven't tried it on, even when I threw myself at you. So, I am going to divulge a lot of stuff that is not normally shared outside of a very small circle."

"I'll try hard not to betray that trust." Whatever was coming, I was going to try to keep it to myself. These people had reached out to me, a stranger, and offered me sanctuary and friendship, I owed them. I picked up a hot savoury pastry and nibbled as Helen got comfortable.

"My name is—"

"Helen, to me you will always be Helen."

"Thank you, Theo. My real, no, my public name has been in the papers many times. I was married to an important public figure. My sister still is, so you will understand the need for me to be able to trust you."

Helen and her elder sister were the children of an upper-middle-class family. A big house, gardens, pool and several expensive cars. Her father was well-known in banking circles. He made enough to have both girls educated at good schools and to take the family on holidays to Europe.

"We were on a beach in the South of France one year, while I was quite young when I noticed that hardly anyone was wearing clothes. I asked Mom what was going on, she replied it was a European thing, did I want to try? I was hesitant. "What if we did it together?" That was good enough for me. From that day on, we always went to nudist beaches, all over Europe."

When they were at home, her Pop had introduced bare bathing in their pool. "Later I worked it out that this was all Pop's idea, especially when some of his friends started to bring their families for pool weekends." Then, Helen explained, one of the neighbors moved, the new people did some landscaping and the pool was no longer private. Pop decided to sell the house and move closer to the city. At the same time, the family had joined a sun club.

The years passed and Helen and her sister, now young women, met a pair of Yale graduates. Both were charming boys, who were on their way to the top. Within two years they were all married. Clarence, Helen's husband, was in finance like Pop, except he was on the ladder to the top. As long as Helen behaved like a dutiful piece of eye candy and the perfect hostess, she was free to do what she wanted, with discretion. Although he didn't come to the 'Country Club' very often, Clarence was happy for her continued membership. Then it all went horribly wrong for them.

One of the Financial Instruments, one that Clarence had encouraged his clients to invest in, fell apart. People were going to lose a lot of money. When the accusations started flying, he rapidly divorced Helen to protect her and her sister and her sister's husband, his former roomy at Yale. The settlement he agreed with Helen included their home and a holiday property in the Hamptons. By the time he had been brought to trial, everything had been settled. Clarence pleaded guilty. After that, all of his remaining, not inconsiderable, assets were seized for the plaintiffs.

"Clarence was sentenced to ten years. He served five and came out a different person. A very different person. We still get on well and Clara is my go-to person for investment advice."

"Ah!" The name change, a different person. I guessed that might be a cause of some reticence on Helen's behalf. "Five years, that was a considerable sacrifice for keeping your names out of the papers!"

"Not that great in the end, an investment possibly."

"Oh?"

"This is the very secret bit. Only six people in the world know this story. I am trusting you with our lives." She looked into my eyes as if looking for some sign, a warning, of betrayal.

"Why?" I interrupted her story, I had to ask the question that had been troubling me since Helen had approached me as I lay by the pool, some six hours ago. "Why are you telling me, a complete stranger, all this?" I decided not to go into the questions about my trustworthiness.

"This place is being strangled, destroyed. We think the Sheriff and his brother want the site back. I, we, don't know why but, they do and they have funds at their disposal." She sipped her wine. "I think you may be what we need to bust this conspiracy open."

A firm of lawyers had sent Oak Leeves Resort several letters, offering to buy the entire place for about seventy-five per cent of the value. The syndicate had declined and set about finding out who was behind the offer.

"Your eyes and ears?" I suggested.

"Yes, and they came up with our not-so-friendly Sheriff." She took a small sip of her wine. Steeling herself to go on, I imagined. "After we declined to offer, things started happening. The access road was blocked for three months by repair works. Works that cut the water supply. We had contractors booked to drill a well for us, and suddenly the water was back.

"Visitors to the resort started being

harassed by the Deputies, doing stop-and-search operations on spurious grounds. Contractors and suppliers suddenly stopped working with the resort. Public complaints were trumped up and the Sheriff would have to investigate, "I am duty bound."

"That must have made it difficult to resist the cash being offered."

"On the contrary, Theo. Every time something happened, we would get a new offer from the lawyers, a lower offer. Fortunately, we have a little bit of political cover, it has been enough to stop the Town Council from forcing us to sell."

"Political cover?"

"Yes, but it is very limited. The State Governor is my brother-in-law, that is why Clarence went to the wall to distance himself from the Candidate-in-waiting all those years back." She continued her narrative.

I discovered that not only was Helen's sister, the State's First Lady. The Governer's wife, I realised, was a former naturist, which could have been disastrous if it had leaked during an election. She had once been a frequent visitor to Oak Leeves; it was a place where she could relax out of the glare of the media spotlight. That would explain the need for secrecy, I now understood about the questions about trust. "So why doesn't she hideaway somewhere else?"

It seemed a simple solution to that issue.

"She could, but how would she see Mom and Pop if she didn't visit?"

"Mom and Pop, do you mean Mary and Greg?" The cards were hitting the table rapidly now.

"Yeah, Pop decided to get out of the 'money game', as he calls it nowadays. I think Clara's brush with the law worried him more than he let on. Oh, and in the interests of full disclosure, Clara is the Governor's Private Financial Policy Advisor. Fortunately, the media have failed to pick that one up too."

Secrets within secrets with a few secrets sprinkled over the top for added sparkle.

"Let me make sure I have all this, "I paused to get my thoughts in order. "I was told you are one of the co-owners of this place, who are the others?"

"Mom and Pop, Mary and Greg, their real names, and my sister has a few thousand invested." Helen hesitated, then guessed at my next question. "Neither the Governor nor Clara has any financial stake in the resort. This is very much a Mom and Pop enterprise."

"An enterprise that the local town Sheriff wants to destroy."

"That's about it, Theo."

"And you hope there is something on my dashcam footage that might be able to get the Brown Brothers to back off?"

Helen nodded. "You mentioned a dog, it gives us an in, to bring more political pressure to bear. As First Lady, my sister is president of the League Against Animal Cruelty, if you have captured Emmet hurting a dog …"

"The power of the State House can be brought into play." I filled in the gap. "Then we had best have a look at the footage."

*****

"Well done you!" Helen threw her arms around my neck and hugged me tightly. It had been a few months, maybe longer, since I had been embraced by a naked woman. I was enjoying the sensation, a little too much perhaps. My body started to react. I eased myself out of the clinch. Helen looked away, as if unsure of why I was backing away. The sparkle in her eyes vanished and she looked away.

"That was as nice as it was unexpected, Helen, but …" Then her lowered eyes saw my burgeoning arousal.

"I'm sorry, I should have thought!" The sparkle reignited in her eyes. "At least it demonstrates that I was right to trust you!"

"So, what's the plan?" There had to be a plan.

"We make copies of that part of the

card. We can use my laptop as the main backup, and another SD card, so we can get it to my sister. If you keep the original, that should do it."

"And if the Sheriff turns up first thing with a warrant, looking for a memory card? We need to have one he can find."

"I don't have a second card, although it would be a good idea. You'll just have to hide the original somewhere safe."

"From what I heard on the radio, Sheriff Brown will have no compunction about tearing the place apart and 'interrogating' me in private." I shuddered at the memory of what some of my Afro-Anerican sources had told me about being questioned by Law Officers in some parts of the South. "Do you know anyone who might have a camera, or even a GPS, with a memory card.?"

"Pop! He had to get a new one for his camera, I'll ask him."

Chapter 5

It was gone midnight when I left Helen's cabin, "Good night, Theo, thank you." Her lips brushed my cheek and I might have felt her nipples touching my chest. Then it might have been a bit of wishful thinking. On my walk back to cabin fourteen, I hid the original memory card, taping it underneath the returned keys box outside the Office.

    I went to bed naked for the first time in years. With just a thin sheet pulled over me, the humidity was just about tolerable and I slept. I had dreamed, but in the morning I was still trying to work out what had happened and where my PJs had gotten to when there was a soft knock on the door. That brought everything, rapidly, to the point of panic. I looked around, desperately, for something to cover my nudity. There it was, on the floor, a towel. Then it clicked, no clothes, a towel, a rustic cabin, Oak Leeves Naturist Resort. My run-in with the Sheriff, a search warrant, a dawn raid, dogs, batons.

    The knock came again, still gentle and undemanding. No sounds of dogs, nor the crackle of radios, it wasn't the Sheriff with his posse. I slipped out of bed, grabbed the towel and hurried to the door. "Who is it?" I whispered.

"It's me, Helen. Do you want some breakfast? Mom is just about to do some bacon and eggs."

Bacon and eggs, just add coffee and you have my attention all day! "Yes, please."

"How do you like your eggs?"

"Hang on," I opened the door, towel still clutched tight to my groin. Helen stood in the early morning sun. Her towel hung casually over her shoulder. I was speechless.

"Eggs?" She asked, "Like your thoughts?"

"Pardon?" I was way off the pace.

"Eggs, scrambled like your thoughts or fried like your brain?" She smiled, all the way from her toes to her eyes.

"Not fair, a beautiful woman wakes me, stands naked in my doorway and expects me to make a choice. How do you like yours?" Follow the leader, it saves thinking.

"Unfertilized." She snickered. "I always wanted to use that line, sadly it's a bit late in life now though."

"Doesn't stop us trying …" It was out of my mouth before my brain had formed the thought.

"Perhaps we should get to know each other a little better first. I'm an easy person when it comes to eggs."

"Bacon, eggs over easy and coffee, please." I was struggling, it had been years since I had been, what? Teased? Flirted with? Given the come-on?

"In the restaurant, about ten minutes? That should give you time for a shower. Pop says he put an emergency guest pack into the bathroom. She waved, just her fingertips, to me and turned away. I couldn't resist and was blowing a kiss. Of course, she looked back at that instant. "Ten minutes!" She smiled again and left me red-faced.

*****

"Hi," Mary greeted me with a smile, put a hand gently on my arm and steered me through the empty dining room. "I have set a table near the window for all of us. We don't normally serve breakfast, it makes the day too long," She explained, noticing my confusion at the lack of customers. "Helen and Greg are just sorting out the package for the mailman to take. "Coffee?"

"Please, Mam."

"Please, Mary. We don't hold with that 'Sir and Mam' crap around here, I ain't the Queen of England!"

"Sorry, Mary. Coffee, black, thank you." Package for the mailman? That made sense, the Sheriff would be a fool to mess with the mail, because that would get the Feds involved.

Helen arrived, sat down opposite me and gave me a huge wink. "Pop said he'll be over as soon as Virgil has gone, Mom. So you can serve up when you are ready" Mary moved back towards the kitchen. "Virgil is the mailman. He'll make sure the camera footage will get to my sister in the next couple of days. Secure, but not very fast, then that is the way it has to be."

"Hello, Greg." I got to my feet as he arrived at the table.

"No need to stand on ceremony, Son." He glanced over at Helen. "So, he knows who we are?"

"Yes, Pop."

"Your sister too?"

"Her role but not her name, Pop," Helen answered respectfully.

"That doesn't take long to find out! A simple search, eh, Marlon?"

"Maybe for Marlon, but I'm Theo while I am here, Greg. I have no internet access and I don't need it for now."

"Good answer, Theo, or should I say,

'Son'."

"Pop!" Helen blushed like a beet.

"Theo is good, Greg," I made a point of stressing his name as opposed to his family title.

"Food's up!" Mary arrived, carrying plates laden with bacon, eggs, sausage, hash browns and grits. As a boy from the Windy City, I'd have forsaken the grits for some toast but I'm in the Carolinas. I'll take one for the team.

"Wow! Looking good!" That was the only thing I could think of to say.

*****

Helen and I were sitting on the veranda that surrounds the office. All was very quiet, we were both letting breakfast and events of the past twenty-four hours digest. Helen was officially on reception duty, so far nothing had disturbed the peace. "It won't be like this tomorrow or Saturday." It was as if she had read my mind. "We are almost overrun come the weekend. I might need to find you somewhere else to sleep if we get very busy."

The terms of my tenancy and the duration of my stay had not been discussed. I had assumed that I would be getting a bill at some point, but how much it would be I had no idea. "Do you get many visitors?". How many nudists were there in this corner of South

Carolina? Or did desperate naturists drive hundreds of miles in search of somewhere safe to enjoy the sun, naked?

"A good weekend, like Labor Day or Fourth of July, with the RV park and all the cabins full, maybe five hundred, plus about the same as day visitors. Sometimes a few more. Membership stands at fifteen hundred."

"That, that is a lot of people. Where do you put them all?" I was flabbergasted.

"The pool gets very busy, we have to put on games and adventures to get the kids away so the adults can have pool time."

"Kids? Kids come here too?"

"From birth to about thirteen years old, then a lot get body conscious and stop coming. Yeah, we get kids! It is a safe environment for them."

"How do you mean, Helen? Safe?"

"Apart from the fact that there are lots of adults looking out for them? Well, any man getting his rocks off looking at children will stick out a mile." An ironic look fixed on her face before I cracked and laughed at the dreadful joke.

"So, what are we going to do after you finish this shift?" I leant back in my chair, the sun felt nice on my face,

"I thought we might find you a pair of

shoes, thongs at least, and I'll show you the rest of the site."

*****

Four hours later, I am lying on my towel, face down while Helen is massaging my factor fifty into my back. We have walked and talked our way around most of the wooded grounds. Now we were in a large clearing. The ground was pretty flat, but from where I was lying, I could see it undulated, forming a regular sort of pattern. "What is the story of this place?" It was different. Things that are different are interesting.

"I really don't know. The area had all been cleared of trees some time while this was still a casino There was some talk that casino management was looking to put in a swimming pool, that might have been here." Helen slapped my butt. "Do you want me to do your front?"

"Are you sure?" I was. I started to roll over, anticipating.

"There you are!" A voice boomed out. It was Duane. "I was sent to warn you that the Sheriff has arrived with a search warrant. The Deputies are going around checking people's IDs."

"Stay here Theo, I'll have to go, the Sheriff will expect to see me. I suggest you hang out here until I get back." She went to kiss me then changed her mind. "Come along

Duane. Let's go and play Sheriff Brown's games."

They disappeared, off back towards the main complex. I went and sat under the trees and thought. There were two, separate, thoughts floating through my mind, Helen and something nagging about the scenario.

I liked thinking about Helen, thoughts of suntan lotion and red wine. The trouble was that every time I thought about Helen, I thought about Oak Leeves, about Oak Lees and the troublesome Sheriff Brown. Why couldn't I just switch off, lay in the sun and think nice thoughts about this attractive woman? What was it that unsettled me? I felt it, something from my past, something not nice that happened in the not-too-recent past was damaging my pleasure in the now. I'd be damned, it would come to me.

"Hey! Theo, it's me! Come on out, they have packed up and gone!"

"Helen! I'm over here." I sat up and waved.

"No, you're not! According to the Visitor's Book, you checked out this morning. You left a comment about having been made welcome and you could get used to swimming without your shorts!" She laughed, "according to Mom you hiked off towards the coast and Fort Sumter, something about retracing your Great, Great Grandpappy's route to join

Beauregard's forces at the start of the War Between the States."

"I'm not sure that my Yankee ancestors would be best pleased by that!" As I said it, a butterfly's wings fluttered deep in my subconscious.

"That thar mae be so, Boy, but yoose in the Carolinahs …" Helen ladled on her Southern drawl "If I dun tell tha Sheriff dat yoose a damn Yankee sympathizer, he ha' the dawgs after y'awl!"

"Hmm, I seem to recall Grandpappy Galpin regaling us boys with tales of his forebear's heroism before he was taken prisoner at Gettysburg."

"Whatever, Pop's family didn't arrive from Canada until 1902, we are of Scottish extraction." That was the first hint of Helen's antecedence.

We wandered back to the pool area, walking so close to each other that our hands brushed from time to time, sending a shock of electricity up my arm. As we approached the beating heart of the resort, I noticed that people were looking at us and smiling. I felt uncomfortable, I looked to Helen for reassurance and felt her hand being extracted from my grip.

"There were more than a few rumors floating around the place after we had dinner last night," Helen whispered, "I think we may have just confirmed them."

"And how do you feel about that?" I knew what I wanted her to say.

"I hate being the subject of rumor." She put her hand on my shoulder and kissed me on the cheek. "I am off, I suppose I had better tell Mom that I have just wound up the bush telegraph."

"Bush telegraph?" I hadn't heard that phrase in years. I knew instantly what it meant but where had I heard it?

"Scuttlebutt," Helen confirmed my understanding. With that, she gave me another peck on the cheek and almost skipped away. Next time, I am going to recognise the tells and get me some lip-to-lip contact!

That was for later; I threw my towel onto a vacant sun bed, rinsed off and dived into the pool. I swam a few lengths, enjoying the feel of the cool, refreshing water rushing across my skin. Then I pulled myself up the steps out of the water. I could feel a dozen pairs of eyes on me as I crashed onto my towel.

"You are a smooth operator, Theo, I'll give you that!"

"Hi, Duane." I recognised the voice. "I don't know about that!"

"Honey, many have tried and many have failed. Princess Elsa has frozen out every man I have seen try." Joannie must have been with him, "Duane is right, you must be one hell of an operator, it's taken you less than a day!".

I prised myself up far enough to see Joannie. "All I was trying to do …" I stopped myself. It wasn't a lack of confidence in Duane and Joannie but… You know the old saw about three can keep a secret, but only if two of them are dead. My secret was shared with six already. I wasn't going to put two more people at risk of incurring the Sheriff's displeasure. "I was just passing by and needed somewhere to rest up. I am following in my Great Great Grandpappy's footsteps to Fort Sumter. He camped out somewhere near here according to his diary." Great Grandpappy Galpin's story was developing all the time.

The Meadow Whispers

Chapter 6

Dinner saw Helen and me at the centre of attention. The rumor mill had hurried the news to the far corners of the resort. If they were hoping for some sort of show, they were out of luck. We had sort of agreed on a protocol. Helen was expecting a heavy day with people arriving early for the weekend. "I need an early night," She had explained. "Ideally one without alcohol. I'm not as young as I used to be, that was why I was quiet at your door first thing."

I had a different reason for not wanting to get involved in anything too physical. I had hoped that Helen would be back from dealing with the Sheriff sooner than she was and had delayed doing my front in anticipation of her return. Now, I knew what Duane had meant about the sun being a bitch on the bits that don't see it very often. I was sore from chest to knees and it was difficult to keep my hands away from the most delicate bits.

"You look like you need a cold shower, followed by plenty of aloe vera lotion massaged into the sore bits!" Helen whispered. We were at a different table to the previous evening, the private one had been reserved for a couple celebrating their anniversary.

"I can live with the cold shower, and the aloe would be good, but I haven't got any."

"I have a few ounces in a bottle back at my place." There was a wicked grin on her lips. "I could do the massage too if you'd like."

"Now, that could be fun …"

*****

It wasn't, not through the want of trying from both of us. "I have heard of burning passion, this is the first time I have encountered it." We had tried several different approaches, I was just too tender. Even kissing it better didn't make it less sore. Although it was fun trying.

"I have melted the Frozen Princess, now she is too hot for my burning love to handle." We had improvised a happy ending.

"Elvis meets Disney, what more could a girl want." She kissed me playfully. "Apart from a full service and fluid change."

"Tomorrow," I promised. If she had demanded something earlier, I reckoned I might have been able to endure …

"That might be better all around." That wicked grin was back.

"Better?"

"Yes, I am on the early shift remember? Tomorrow, we can take our time." She dragged her hair across my chest. It tingled but the agony of a few hours' past was gone. "Now go back to your chalet and let me get my beauty sleep."

"You don't need it, you are —"

"That might be because I always get my sleep. You are going to need a good night's rest too. You have a lot on."

"No, I haven't." I didn't even have the sneakers I escaped from the Dodge on.

"True, but you have things to do tomorrow," I raised my James Bond eyebrow. "Before that! You will need to bring your stuff over here and get your chalet ready for the people arriving after lunch."

Well, I had known I would probably have to move out of fourteen, I hadn't been expecting to move in with a woman I hadn't met forty-eight hours earlier. "Yes, Mam!" We kissed.

On the doorstep, Helen surprised me by announcing very loudly, "Thank you, Theo. That fridge rattling all the time was driving me mad!" Then she leant forward and kissed me on each cheek, continental style. "That'll confuse the gossips!" She whispered as she pulled back.

*****

Sleep didn't come quickly. I lay there in the dark, lamenting not using the factor fifty earlier.

I ran the other events of the day through my mind, ending with the very European 'between friends' kiss. The final tumbler fell into place, Europe.

*****

In the last years of the old millennium, I got been contracted by a news agency to cover the US contribution to the cleanup after the Yugoslavian civil wars. I had arrived in Europe early and took a bit of a road trip. Well, you would want to see Paris and Rome at least, wouldn't you? I saw lots of *bisous* being exchanged, even between the young men when couples met.

From Rome I was moved to the former Yugoslavia, still a hotbed of racial hatred. Then one afternoon, I was on a patrol with an American unit, part of NATO's Implementation Force (IFOR), near Srebrenica, we came across a group of local women. They were digging fresh graves in the remains of the destroyed village graveyard. They claimed to have found the burial site of the village men who had been taken away in the summer of 1995 and never seen again.

The women guided us to a clearing on a wooded hillside. There were several open graves, the women had started to exhume the bodies. "You have the remains of six or seven men here, why are you digging dozens of new graves?" Journalist, I ask questions, in this case via our local interpreter.

He refused to ask the question. Instead, he pointed to the clearing floor, "See the dents and humps spread right across the ground." I looked, looked again then picked up the pattern of indentations. I nodded. "Each of the indentations marks the graves of maybe a dozen men. The victims were shot in small groups. The ones not killed were forced to dig a grave, throw their friends' bodies into the hole and cover them with soil. The next day, another group of men would be snatched from the villages. Yesterday's grave diggers were the first to be murdered today. The cycle continued for many days."

"How do you know that?" I was shocked, I was struggling to comprehend.

"Two of us ran. They killed Reuf. I was wounded. In the night, I managed to crawl into the hedge around the field. Three days later the murderers, their work done, left. I crawled to a nearby house and, well here I am."

"As the bodies decay, Sir," One of the grunts came to our rescue. "They shrink and the soil over them collapses into the space."

*****

It was such a horrific incident that I had blanked it out. Until earlier today, I hadn't accessed that memory since I left Bosnia. Did this mean …? I could barely countenance the thought; unmarked graves, tens of them.

But, if they were graves, who was in them?

"Stories of vehicles with New York plates arriving late at night and disappearing before dawn," I remember being told, was it only last night? Pa Brown had vanished. There were loans unpaid. Gambling, drugs and prostitution. It all shouted The Mob.

I wasn't going to get any sleep, so I decided I might as well follow the logic trail and see where it led.

Pa Brown's casino business had just taken a massive cash flow hit. His original backers, or were they partners? in the 'enterprises' that he had been forced to close? No matter. Suppose, The Mob had offered to forgive the loan repayments in exchange for somewhere to hide the bodies.

I eventually dozed off before reaching any definitive answers. Besides, dreaming of Helen was a much more pleasing pastime.

Chapter 7

The sun was streaming in through the gap where the blinds hadn't been drawn properly. I was in that nice, dreamy state, planning the day. The knock on the door was no surprise, I'd been waiting. I leapt out from under the thin sheet and bounded across the room to open the door. Helen stepped inside and we kissed.

"So, what's the story, morning glory?" She laughed. I looked down and I felt my face heat up. "Later, big boy! It is nice to know that I still have that effect. Last night didn't put you off?" I was still too embarrassed to speak. "Just be careful not to get burnt again, today!"

I gave up fighting it and gave her a smack on the derrière. "Naughty! Don't tease, it is not nice."

"It looks nice enough to eat from here!" She smiled and licked her lips.

"Haven't you got work to go to?" If she had said 'no'… but she didn't.

"I'll be off at one o'clock, lunch at mine?"

"If I'm through with my packing. Plus! I have to clean and tidy this place first." I can tease too.

*****

I had got done packing up my gear, well my running shoes, a baggie half filled with toiletries and the book I was still reading were out on one of the chairs on the veranda. The other chair was groaning under the weight of my laundry, not. I stripped the bedding off the mattress and added it to the laundry pile. Then with the room empty, I swept through, moving the furniture as I went.

That was when I found the body. The bedside cabinet can't have been moved for weeks. The mouse was little more than a clump of fur and a few bones. I swept the remains into the dustpan and took them to the dumpster.

On the way back I went to the linen store to collect the change of bedding and bathroom towels. I grabbed myself a new pool towel too. Hopefully, one way or another it would be the last I would need to borrow. I had another piece of the jigsaw, one that fitted with the scenario developing in my mind.

I made the bed and laid the bathroom towels on the bed covers, the way they had been when I checked in. Outside, I threw my fresh pool towel over my shoulder, picked up the dirty linen and my personal items and headed over to the laundry. I dropped the dirty sheets and pillowslips into their respective baskets and went to dump the rest of my stuff over at Helen's place.

It was still too early for lunch. I slathered sun protection all over my shoulders and front, paying careful attention to the delicate areas from the day before. Then I hiked off towards the poolside, towel and book in hand.

"Look who's strolling around looking like he belongs?" Duane shouted to Joannie on the sunbed next to where he was doing a crossword puzzle.

"What are you shouting about now?" Joannie pulled her headphones off of her ears. "My story is just getting interesting."

"I was just saying to Theo here, he seems to have settled in nicely."

"Hi, to you too Duane, and to you Joannie." I smiled and waved. I should have expected some sort of teasing after being seen in Helen's company so often. "I need to finish my book! So, I thought I'd get comfortable before the crowds arrive."

As I settled into a chair, my back was unprotected by sunburn stuff, it struck me just how comfortable I was. It was barely forty-eight hours since I had lucked out at the gate to the … resort. I had been thinking nudist colony, but since then I might have become a naturist. I had enjoyed swimming with nothing on.

Walking about in the open air was easier without sweaty clothes sticking to me. I was even sitting here in mixed company with my, slightly burnt, equipment on display and hardly giving it a thought.

I went back to trying to read my book. Eventually, I put it down. Ok, so I threw it on the ground in disgust. I just couldn't cope with the story once it twisted to get into eugenics, something the author seemed to be in favour of.

"It had the same effect on me!" Duane had snuck up on me, he had a book in his hand. "John Ball, his follow up to In the Heat of the Night, Virgil Tibbs? The movie starred Sidney Poitier?"

"Gotcha, didn't Poitier get an Oscar for his role?"

"Something like that. This is the second book in the series. It could be you in the title, you have proved yourself to be 'The Cool Cottontail', except you don't look much like Tibbs!" He laughed.

I took the book and read the blurb on the cover. "I'll give it a go, thanks, Duane."

"No problem, any friend of Helen's is good with me. As long as they don't … but then you won't, will you?" He walked back towards Joannie, who was sitting eyes closed, headphones clamped over her ears. I was left to pick the veiled threat out of his words.

The Cool Cottontail was certainly a book of its time, big sedans, with fins, soft suspension and big V-8s with tires that squealed at every turn. John Ball had the language skills to create wonderful images; I'm a wordsmith, I know these thin … What the hell?"

Something cool and soft touched my back as a kiss landed on my head. Helen stood just behind my chair, grinning like the Cheshire Cat in Alice.

"I see your book is more interesting than I am!" I glanced at my watch. "Don't worry, I got off early. Greg told me to come and tell you the news."

"What news?"

"We have decided to let you work off your bill. You have a shift guiding newcomers around the site tomorrow." It must be very well paid, working here, I thought. "And on Sunday, we would like you to check the cabins before returning the cleaning deposits," She continued. The good news? I was wanted until Sunday!

"If I am going to be acting as a guide tomorrow, I'll need a refresher tour! Would now be a good time? I am not sure what people have planned for me this afternoon!" My grin was reflected back to me in her expression.

*****

I was trailing my fingers gently along the spine of the sleeping woman whose head rested on my chest. I hadn't the energy to move anymore. I had been scheduled to undertake a tour that had explored the nooks and crannies of Oak Lees Naturist resort. Instead, Helen and I had indulged in a detailed exploration of each other. A voyage of discovery I wanted to repeat, perhaps a little slower so I had time to appreciate the finer points.

I became aware that Helen was only pretending to be asleep. Her eyes were averted and she was keeping very still apart from a single finger gently stroking my thigh. I responded, by squeezing her bottom gently with my right hand. She looked up. I pulled her upward into an embrace and we kissed.

"Was that good for you?" She whispered the question. I almost laughed.

"Let's just say if I was physically capable, we would be making love right now. It surpassed last night's dreams." I kissed her again, a promise for later.

"Are you sure?"

Self-doubt? From the most competent woman, I had met in a long time? From an attractive woman, I have hardly been able to tear my eyes away from? "Oh, I couldn't be more sure, but why are you asking? Did I fail to light your fire?"

"You lit my fire all right, I think I am still smoking … but I'm not sure that I am very good at this."

"Oh?"

"Look at my history, my ex-husband was never that enthusiastic and then he decided to become a woman. The few encounters I have had since have been rather short, rushed affairs. So, I started to think I wasn't very good."

"Ha! That is as far from the truth as you can get! As Joannie boasted to Duane the other day, she is the one that makes him quick!" I kissed her on the nose and found a little energy from somewhere.

*****

We set off to do the tour training in the late afternoon sun. We were attracting stares, followed by nudges and whispered comments. We were walking together and holding hands, we couldn't help it. The expression on my face must have made me look like the dog-with-two-tails-who-had-just-caught-the-cat-that-got-the-cream. The cat looked pretty happy about things too.

I discovered that there were four shower blocks, each surrounded by power hookups for ten RVs. There were another couple of blocks set back in the rear-lot areas of the site for those who enjoy camping out in tents. I now understood why Helen and her family wanted to build a second pool.

"Didn't you realise the pool wasn't going to be big enough when you took on the land?" We were sitting on top of a small hill overlooking one of the camping areas where the first pup tent was being pitched by a young couple.

"We had hoped it wouldn't be big enough. We always planned to expand the facilities when the membership grew. It all happened rather faster than we expected." Helen paused, collecting her thoughts. "Pops, Greg, had concerns we might overstretch ourselves and end up having to dance to the bank's tune. With both Pops and Clara having been in the money game, Mom and I accepted their wisdom. Which, based on where we are now, was sound advice."

"Is that because of Sheriff Brown?"

"You got it, the lawyer's letter and all the rest. They put the brakes on our plans big time. Thanks to Pops' caution we are able to do more than survive."

"Oh?" I thought I might be on the edge of prying too deeply, but a journalist does what a journalist does.

"Having to restrict our plans to expand the resort has been a benefit too. We can almost charge what we want for people to come here. Membership is a precious commodity; it is limited to fifteen hundred. As long as fifteen hundred and one people are willing to pay the price, we can charge what we like. The same with day visitors and casual campers, we use price to control numbers. Because we manage the number of people on the site, we can manage our staff needs to minimize the payroll and food budget. We run a profitable business even if we are underutilizing our acreage."

"Sounds like you have a nice little Mom and Pop business going here."

"It is OK, Theo. Just it isn't what we wanted to do twelve years ago when we started to work on this."

"All right, Helen, talk to me about the plans you had when your family took over this place."

Helen talked, I listened, and occasionally I asked questions to steer the conversation.

The site of the Brown family casino had stood empty for over a year before Pops became aware of it. He was looking for real estate for "investment" purposes. He had decided to get out of the rat race before the rats caught him. He wanted a retirement project that would allow him to get out of his business suit and into his 'one-button suit.'

Helen had pointed to my belly button to make sure I got the 'one-button suit' reference.

He was able to secure the land. Helen had come in with the money from her divorce settlement. That was to contribute to the costs of clearance and redevelopment of the area. It was going to be an expensive project.

There are shabby little campgrounds and expensive resorts for naturists across the country. Pops' vision was to build a high-quality naturist resort for the masses. The family were going to enable people from all walks of life to come and enjoy being at one with nature. They were going to make people who could only afford a pup tent as welcome as the millionaires wanting luxury accommodation. It was a huge long-term plan!

Then, instead of being able to expand, they were threatened, obstructed and put under pressure to sell at a loss.

"The Sheriff and his backers must want the land back for some reason." I was trying to work around to confirming or eliminating my late-night theory. "Have they ever offered to buy part of the site?" For instance that meadow, I wondered silently.

"No, it has always been the whole acreage."

Shame, I had probed hoping for a lead as to which area of land they had wanted, and with it a clue to their motive. "Is thar gold in them thar hills?" I pointed around as I asked,

I'm not very good at silly voices. I should give up trying.

"Nobody has ever said anything."

"Did you get any geological work done as part of your due diligence process before buying the land?"

"Theo, if you are thinking that we might be sat on a multi-million-dollar oil well or something, you are sadly mistaken." That wasn't an answer to the question I'd asked, my frustration must have shown on my face. Helen continued, "But to answer your question, no, we didn't. There was no history of problems with the land."

"There must be something of value on the land that they want. Maybe there is pirate treasure or something similar buried somewhere and they want it back?" I left the thought hanging.

"And because we have fenced off the whole parcel they can't get to it?" Helen was a bright cookie, that's why I love her. What did I just say? … "Then, they didn't start with the lawyers and intimidation until we had been running for several years. It can't be that, surely?"

"Can you remember what else changed about that time? A new Town Mayor? A newly elected Council? Some proposed development?" Did I just think what I think I just thought? After two failed marriages, I'd promised myself ...

"There had been elections a year before, I think there was a change of leadership of the library, nothing significant." She shook her head, I watched the golden light shimmering in her blonde hair. "As for a new development? You have been into town, what development? I think they had to put together a Planning Committee to consider our ... Our plans! That was when it started. We submitted an outline plan for new accommodations, a recreation hall and that second pool. We wanted to make sure that we weren't wasting money on getting architects and engineers in for a project that was doomed before it started."

"That might be significant." I reached out and pushed a few strands of her hair back behind her ear. A little gesture that ended our conversation and led to our lips being otherwise engaged.

*****

The light had changed from golden to orange, "Time for us to get back." Helen started to her feet. "I need to make sure you don't waste away, now that I have found you." She added in a half-whisper.

I was getting hungry but I was more interested in decoding the second part of that sentence. Did it mean what I hoped it meant?

"Your place or the restaurant?" I asked as I let Helen help me to my feet.

"It will have to be Cheeks, we have eaten the cupboard bare. I don't often eat at home, no point when I eat at Cheeks for nothing." She smiled. Her whole face smiled and shone in the light of the setting sun. Her words "now that I've found you," chased my earlier "that's why I …" thought around in circles in my head as we walked, arm in arm, back towards the centre of the resort.

I had been vaguely aware of an increase in the number of RVs we had passed, but it wasn't until the hubbub of voices from the bar hit me, that I realised that the resort was starting to fill. The jacuzzi that had stood bubbling to itself a few hours before was now occupied by naked people, laughing and shouting jokes to each other. Other groups of chairs were covered with the towels of conversing couples.

As we walked past, I could feel the draught created by the turning heads and swiveling eyes. "Hey, Princess, who is the lucky man?" He was taller, wider, and better looking than me and in great physical shape. "You could have had me. What's so special about him?"

"Beyond the fact he isn't married, do you mean, Tex? Or has divorce number five come through now? Gales of laughter followed us through the doors into the dining room.

The Meadow Whispers

Ted Bun

Chapter 8

"I guess you will have seen the pool as you drove in." If they hadn't, it was front and centre from where I was standing, pointing out the layout of Oak Leeves' facilities to Lee and Susi. "The shallow end is towards the clubhouse, bar and Cheeks restaurant. The sports area, the horseshoe pitch, the pickle-ball court and the mini-golf course are just beyond the deep end."

I had been asked about the pool depth by Mo and Cathy, who had three kids under seven with them. "Only the two of them are mine." Cathy laughed "The neighbors back home lent us their son, so they can enjoy a date weekend" I managed to stop my jaw from dropping. I was still getting used to the idea of people bringing their kids to a place full of naked people. I hadn't considered that they might bring other people's offspring too.

"Oh?" Was all I could muster by way of response.

"We normally all go down to a place in Florida, but I suppose it is no secret that the neighbors are having a few problems, so here we are," Mo explained.

"Florida? Why do you go that far?" I'd seen the South Carolina plates on their RV.

"Cathy here is a State Employee and worried about being recognised, so we would travel for hours to relax au natural. What with the kids having gotten to an age where they get antsy if they are strapped in for that long, something had to change."

"Yeah, well Mo convinced me that the only people who could see me 'galivanting around in the skinny' would have to be in the resort and, by default, in the same state of undress. So, here we are!"

"Sorry, Cathy, I hadn't meant to pry. Mo was asking about the pool, it's two foot six at the shallow end." I pointed. "The deep end is seven foot deep, so take care diving. You don't want to try it at the wrong end!" Mo laughed, I was out of my hole.

Lee and Suzi were benefiting from my earlier *faux pas*, it wasn't only kids who needed to know the pool layout. How embarrassing having to ask if you are a non-swimmer. It cost me nothing to repeat the diving-in joke I'd had with Mo. In fact, I was learning more about real people by doing this job than I had in my years of journalism.

As a journalist, I get to meet and talk to lots of people. Sadly, most of them have an agenda. They want somebody arrested and put in prison. They are trying to deflect the blame onto others. They are trying to minimize their wrongdoing. They are trying to draw attention to themselves. A hundred and one reasons to try to get the journalist to look in a specific direction, not at the truth.

Today, the people I had been talking to were, in the main, only wanting to find out how to make the most of their time at Oak Leeves. I was surprised that many more wanted to know where the restrooms were in relation to the pool, or where they could get a shower near the jacuzzi than there were wanting to know how to get to the bar. I'd like to think it was my riveting exposition, but it was more likely to be because it didn't open until lunchtime.

*****

"How did it go?" I was relaxing with a beer. Sat out on the balcony of Helen's chalet when she returned from her stint booking visitors in. I stood up to welcome her home. It was several minutes before I answered her question.

"It was really good. I was nervous when I started, but I soon realised that I knew more than the guests and they nearly all had the same questions. After that, I was able to relax. Once I got going, I thoroughly enjoyed being helpful."

"Ah, but tomorrow you get to play the bad guy. We have a couple of youngsters who are going to check the RVs and campers have left their emplacements clean and tidy. Mary wants you to do the inspections of the chalets. You know the sort of thing, making sure that they have been left clean and tidy with nothing missing. You get the job because there have been a few instances of people bullying the younger, less experienced workers. She expects that you will be able to stand up to people who try it on. 'No clean, no refund!' It is that simple. We have to use unrefunded money to pay for people to do the job."

*****

The view from the balcony when we settled down to watch, was one of a resort at its limit. The pool was crowded, they weren't going to be playing water polo during the afternoon. The horseshoe pitching contest had drawn a large number of players and an even larger number of spectators. I guessed that bets were being taken judging by the groans and excited cheering coming from that direction.

Over towards the camping field, I could see thin whisps of smoke rising. I pointed them out to Helen.

"It will be the Campers Cookout, they set up a few grills and everyone who wants to join in drags a cooler full of beer and food over to the area and share and share alike. You'd think it would get messy, waste food, paper plates and empty beverage container all over the place, but no. That crowd seem to self-police pretty effectively. I guess it is because they are regulars in the main and like to think of themselves almost as stakeholders in the place." I nodded my understanding.

On the terrace outside the bar, every table was taken. I could see the waitresses dashing back and forth with orders. They were easy to spot, they were the only ones wearing clothes, well long t-shirts, I suspected that the girls had underwear of some sort on underneath. I had seen a young guy in speedos pulling on one of the orange t-shirts early this morning. I was only looking in his direction in an effort to read the writing on the back. 'Staff. Like you, we dress for work!" That made sense. I commented on the words to Helen.

"Yes, the dark orange text on the paler shirts works nicely. We used to give them white shirts but that had unintended consequences; spills and such like."

"Ah! Accidental wet t-shirt competitions?"

"Except the girls weren't volunteers. We tracked down the instigators pretty quickly, they are on our, thankfully short, list of unwelcome visitors. Then we changed to the colored shirts, you see today, to remove temptation."

"Shrewd move, I'm surprised you can get staff at all."

"Remember what I said about children getting modest and stopping coming with their folks?" I nodded. "Well, they turn into college students. College students need to earn money and we pay quite well. The kids that stopped coming, know we employ clothed servers, and they have seen it all before. Plus, we offer a safe place to work. Unlike many other bars and restaurants where they may have worked, they know that patting and pinching is an absolute no-no here. Some of them even bring friends along. Anyhow, the message gets back to the colleges and we get a steady stream of youngsters asking if they can come and work here. Even if they prefer to keep their clothes on, they know what they are getting into!"

"Wow, I wouldn't have imagined that would happen."

"You'll see at the end-of-season staff party, especially if the weather is good."

Had I just been invited to an event? One that doesn't happen for months? "Does this mean I am Staff now?"

"By the way, your clean tee shirt is on the counter in the kitchen, ready for you to wear tomorrow!"

"Best I get a good night's sleep then!"

"I think it might work better if you were sleep deprived and grumpy. You'll be less willing to put up with excuses if you are bad-tempered after not getting enough sleep,"

Helen laughed, as she pulled me towards the bedroom door.

*****

"Hi Theo, I've got the people from chalet number fourteen here, they say it is ready to go. Can you see if it is as good as when you left it, please?" Mary's voice cut clearly through the crackling and hissing of the radio's static. I supposed that using handheld walkie-talkies made sense. I was only a few hundred yards from the office but walking backwards and forwards would have slowed things down. I could imagine the time and energy wasted running to and from the RV park and the campground would be ridiculous. As for dialling all the relevant mobile phone numbers trying to find someone who was free.

"I'll be there in five, Mary. Seven is clear to go."

"Copy that, Theo. Then, they always take care of the place." A few seconds delay, then she was on to the girls out on the RV park. "Anybody in the RVP, A3 is ready to roll. Do I have a taker?"

"Mary, it's Dulcie I'm here already. Frank and Chrissie have cleared up good. They are moving up to the holding park. You can release their deposit." And on it went.

I found that there were two distinct groups, one left the place as if nobody had even stepped across the threshold. The others were happy to pay for cleaning, accepting the loss. Even though the deposit was enough to pay for five hours of work. None of the rooms I saw was that bad I couldn't have sorted it in a few hours.

I was finished just after midday. "You are all done, Theo," Mary's voice crackled through the ether. "Go get yourself some refreshment. Good job!"

I didn't need to be told twice. I headed to the bar. It wasn't as busy as yesterday and soft drinks were the order of the day. I got a glass of diet Dr Pepper and stood in a corner, where I listened in on the conversations.

"What's the betting I get tested this week?"

"I got stopped by one of the Deputies last time. Breath test and a look in the back, I was on my way in five minutes."

"That was a Deputy, they don't give …"

"Ladies in the room!"

"…they don't give two hoots. The Sheriff, on the other hand, now he had me held up while he searched for open bottles!"

I felt guilty, I knew that the searches would be redoubled because the Sheriff would still be looking for me. At that moment the shutter fell away from my eyes. I knew why I had been put to work this weekend. As I said before, Helen, and I suspect her whole family, are smart cookies. They had hidden me in plain sight, dressed up in an orange tee, one of their staff. Nobody remembers the staff. Most people don't even see the staff. I'd been told some amazing stories by hotel workers over the years.

I finished my drink and decided to head back to Helen's place to hide out there, and maybe have a few of the snacks people had left behind. Some people had vacated leaving the place spotless, except for a few unopened packs and drinks sitting on the table. I wasn't going to starve.

> *"I've gone to Kroger's to get some provisions, I should be back about two, I'll bring lunch. Take it easy and get some rest. I want you fit and raring to go! H xxx"*

Shopping? It wasn't as if we needed food or drink. There was a bar and a pretty darn good restaurant a few steps away from the front door. There was bound to be a reason, I decided that maybe I should go with her suggestion.

*****

The next thing I remember is being bounced awake and almost off the bed. Before I was over the shock I was being kissed. I just hope it is Helen, otherwise, someone else has got hold of the key to the place!

"A man who does what he's told. You'll make some woman a wonderful husband!"

"I know two women who might disagree with you, Helen, my love!" Oops, that word again and this time I said it out loud.

"Ha! Idiots both! You know how to make me happy." I think the word might have penetrated her cerebral cortex. She went silent for a second, before she commanded, "Make me happy, right now, Theo! Make me happy!"

I did my best; I think I might have succeeded. It took a while and all of my energy but in the end, she sighed contentedly, her head resting on my chest. My nose buried in her damp hair, inhaling her scent mingled with the fruity aroma of her shampoo. I was enjoying the gentle pulling sensation as her fingers pushed through the hairs on my chest.

"I have some news," She whispered.

"I hope it is good news," I said, lifting my face away from her blonde locks.

"I hope it is too!" Helen wriggled around until she was sitting upright, looking me in the face. "I spoke to my sister. I used the call box outside the supermarket to call her."

"Ah! I wondered why it was necessary to go shopping today."

"Yeah, a set routine, just to keep in touch. She is coming to Oak Lees to have a word about animal cruelty tomorrow. She wants you to be available when she meets with the Sheriff. So, you will be free to leave after that."

I knew one day I would have to leave the resort. I hadn't planned on it being tomorrow, or any time soon. "One slight problem," I grasped at the first straw I saw, "apart from a slightly sweaty orange tee, I don't have any clothes!"

"I bought some chinos while I was in the store, elasticated waist but I don't know your exact size and a couple of casual shirts."

"Are you trying to get rid of me, Helen?" I got no response. She had broken eye contact with me. "I was kinda hoping to be allowed to stay around a while longer. I have gotten the hang of this nudity thing and I was … Well, thank you for getting me some clothes."

"I'm glad you have relaxed into the lifestyle here, Theo. I hope you'd like to come and visit us again." Her eyes were still averted. I put my hand under her chin and lifted her tear-streaked face so I could look her straight in the eyes.

"Who told you I wanted to leave this place? To leave you?"

"You came here to hide from the Sheriff. We have had some fun. The Sheriff is about to get his comeuppance. Why would you stay?"

"Because..." I was about to say, I don't know what I was about to say. What came out was "I think I have fallen in love with you!"

"You think? Are sure you aren't just confusing your heart with ... with your groin?"

"I might be, Helen." Honesty. I had promised myself I would always be truthful with women. That was at the same time as I swore off women. "I might be but there is only one way to find out, I'd like to hang around a bit longer to make sure. I also have a theory about why people want you off this piece of real estate. I want to research it a bit, if I may."

"So, you want to hang around naked, sleeping with me, while you put a new story together?"

"No, I want to discover who is behind the bid to destroy your family business. To find a way to get them to leave you and your family alone and prove to you ... and as importantly to me, that I love you!"

Chapter 9

Things were a little cool between Helen and me the following morning. We both were lost in our private thoughts. I had refused to reveal my theories about what, and who lay behind the problems that Oak Leeves faced. I had used the 'I' word several times.

"So you say!" I can only assume that others had told her that too, on her road to becoming Elsa, the Princess with the frozen heart.

After a frosty breakfast, Helen announced that she had work to do in the office and left me to it. I took my book and towel to the pool. It was quiet, even Joannie and Duane had disappeared with the weekend crowd. I wondered if they had checked out.

I swam a few laps. I read a few pages. I tried hard to disengage my brain. It wouldn't stop. Conversations from the previous evening looped around in my thoughts. I changed a word here, an emphasis there, and we laughed. But I hadn't, and the reality played again.

"Get your new clothes on, Theo." It was Helen and I was still Theo. The name Marlon had been cast like an obscenity several times the previous evening. "Someone is coming for us. Oh, and bring the original memory card with you."

That was it! Where the coolness had begun, my feeble joke about not being able to leave the resort because I had no clothes. I should have begged her, 'don't make me, I want to stay, I don't want to leave, please!' But I hadn't, I'd opened my mouth and put my foot right into it!

"On my way!" I glanced at my watch; it was a little after midday. I wasn't hungry.

*****

A visitor was waiting at the gate, a female. I never had any doubts she was a Secret Service Agent, even before she introduced herself, "Agent Jones." I am one of the team assigned to protect the state's First Lady. Helen and I introduced ourselves by our real names. It was the first time I had heard it, instantly I knew who her ex-husband was. I sat in the back of the car and kept quiet. Helen got into the front seat of the big, black SUV.

"I thought it would be late afternoon before you would need him." Helen flicked a glance in my direction.

"The Sheriff must have been stressed out." Agent Jones kept her eyes on the road as she spoke. "He completely overstepped the mark. He snatched the memory card out of the First Lady's hand and stamped on it, deliberately trying to destroy the evidence.

As a result, we were able to bring in the State Law Enforcement Division. They have the power to arrest a Sheriff." I already knew that little gem. "He has been read his rights and they are holding him in his office. They are waiting for an Agent from the South Carolina Bureau of Investigation to arrive to question him."

At least he wasn't in a position to arrest me, let alone claim I had been resisting arrest to explain my bruises. Agent Jones was still talking.

"His idiot brother threw a punch at my colleague, Agent Smith, during questioning. So, we have the FBI on the way too."

These Secret Service Agents are Federal employees and assaulting a Government Officer in the course of his, or her, duty would be a Federal matter.

I sat at the back of the SUV, trying to work out how many Agencies were now involved in what had started as a case of animal cruelty. The Sheriff's office, the Secret Service, the FBI, the SCBI and the SC Law Enforcement Division, all had a stake in the case. Meanwhile, the two women in the front seats studiously ignored me.

*****

There were a lot of cars outside the Sheriff's Office. Other than the Sheriff's car, the Black and Whites were only noticeable by their absence. I suppose the Deputies had discovered that they were better able to protect and serve the community by being out and about. Besides, it might be safer for themselves, and the Sheriff, if they were unavailable to answer questions.

"Mr Gates?" A solid man in a dark suit shook my hand. "I'm Agent Smith, I just wanted to shake the hand of the man who did to Emmet Brown what duty stopped me from doing!" I noticed a slight bruise on the man's left cheek.

"The dog abuser you mean?" Smith nodded. "I understand how much restraint it must have taken." Until this was all over, I wasn't admitting anything! "Judging by that mark," I pointed to my right cheek to mirror Smith's face, "So, Mr Brown assaulted a Federal employee, which I understand means that it is an FBI case."

"You are well informed, Mr Gates."

"I think what Mr Gates is saying, is that he would like a word with the FBI about extending their investigation, if you could pass on the message, Agent Smith," Helen intervened.

"Would you care to enlighten me about why I would want to facilitate that, Mam?"

"I think that if you were to tell the First Lady that I was suggesting it as a course of action, she would recommend that you followed it up."

I stayed silent. I was trying hard to protect my sources, even if they were hardly talking to me.

*****

"OK, Mr Gates, what is this all about?" The Fed had been reading something on his laptop, I had waited quietly until he finished and closed the lid. "You don't appear to have any previous connections with the people in this investigation." It must have been my record he had been looking through.

"I have suspicions that Oak Leeves stands on the site of a major criminal conspiracy. One that almost certainly crosses State boundaries. It probably has an international element too. I presume that puts any investigation firmly in the Bureau's remit."

"I'm listening, Mr Gates." He pulled the cap off his pen and placed it on a notepad.

"OK, I am going to start back at the beginning, before the Union was established." I held up my hand to stop his interruption. "Some of this is in the FBI files, but I want us both to start in the same place, so we only have to go through it once."

"Go on then … but keep it short."

I recounted the history of the colonial French control of the territory. How the area had been missed when the rest of the French holdings were transferred to the newly independent America. The anomaly that the Brown family had recognised and exploited. I told the tale of the end of the casino, "This should be in the Bureau's files." Then I moved on to the new owners' plans and how suddenly there was money to buy the land back.

"Interesting, but where are we going with this?" The Fed looked at the few notes he had taken. "There is nothing there for us!"

"That's the way the "conspiracy" wanted things to stay, below the horizon, until the Oak Leeves' owners gave up and sold the real estate to them." The Fed was putting the cap back on his pen. "Then I was forced to hide out at the resort. While being shown around, I saw something that disturbed a memory I had deliberately hidden away. I came across an area of meadow, the site of a proposed new pool for the resort. The surface of which resembled a field of mass graves I witnessed in the former Yugoslavia." Judging by his reaction, the Fed had seen that assignment in my file. I pressed on to my conclusion. "We have the scene of a less than legal enterprise, with possible mob involvement. We have a segment of that scene that reminds me of a burial ground. For years all is peaceful, the sleeping dog lies in the warm sun, until someone disturbs its slumbers, threatening to dig up its bones." I chose that word carefully.

"Bones? Have you seen any bones, Mr Gates?"

"I haven't got access to tools like Ground Penetrating Radar to carry out a survey without digging. I didn't want to go contaminating your evidence, so digging on the site was not on my agenda."

"Thank you for that. How sure are you about your conclusion? I am going to have to go out on a limb to get the funding for this!"

"If I had a hundred thousand dollars to my name, I'd invest it in a GPR sweep!" My conviction was evident in my voice.

I was released from the interview room soon after. As I closed the door, I heard the man from the FBI on his phone. Out in the reception area, I was surprised to see Helen talking to a petite redhead. I looked closely and could see no family resemblance. The radio behind the reception desk buzzed. The redhead excused herself and put on a set of headphones.

"Hi, Carl … Nope and the Feds are here too now … OK, I'll mark you down as off duty. Don't forget you are first on call this evening!" No wonder I couldn't see any family resemblance. I was a little shocked that I hadn't noticed the Deputy's uniform she was wearing. Was that a side effect of spending time with people who don't wear clothes?

"So, what did the FBI have to say then, Marlon?" I picked up the message that Helen was still not happy.

"Not a lot, he listened to my theory and asked a few questions." I tried to change the course of the conversation. "Is she part of your eyes and ears in the town?" I indicated the redhead, who was still talking on the radio.

"Yep, not all of them, but she is an important part of the network. What is going to be happening next?"

"I don't know, I wasn't told. Has anybody mentioned …" I was going to say 'my stuff' but I caught that foot on its way into my mouth. "Lunch? I'm getting very hungry."

"Sorry, Mr Gates," I turned to face the redhead. "I should have said earlier, The Secret Service lady said we were to get you a sandwich or something from Bella's but to wait here for them to be delivered."

"Thanks! What's Bella's special?"

"They do a great hot chicken sandwich, but seeing as you are from the North, I'm told the pastrami on rye is the best south of the Potomac!"

"What do you think, Princess" I had identified that I didn't know which name to use for Helen.

"I'm a sucker for her hot chicken, Marlon. How about we take one of each and we can swap halfway?" A lot of the tension dropped out of her face, I must have played the name thing right. Then it occurred to me why I had been Marlon since we got in the SUV. It was my real name and Helen was using it to emphasize the need for caution about her family name.

The redhead was phoning the order over to the restaurant when the FBI agent appeared from the interview room. Now, Ma'am," He addressed Helen. "I'd like a quick chat with you. We should be done before that food is delivered."

"I need a quick comfort break first, then I'll be right with you." She gave me a strained smile and disappeared to the restroom. The Fed avoided eye contact with me and returned to the interview room.

The redhead was engaged in some local tittle-tattle with whoever had taken the order. So, I went and sat down on one of the chairs against the far wall. I looked at the posters and fidgeted. Far sooner than I had expected, the door opened, our food delivery I hoped. A woman came in, I knew from the way she was dressed she wasn't our sandwich delivery person. She was wearing a pair of tailored slacks, a matching jacket and a pair of smart flat-heeled shoes. A businesswoman I assumed.

She strode over to the counter, just in time for the redhead to signal her to wait as she picked up the phone. The businesswoman half turned, looking around the office. 'I know you,' I thought, but I couldn't place her. The face was familiar but …

Phone call over, the redhead transferred her attention to the waiting businesswoman.

"Watson, Cathy Watson, State Bureau of Investigation. I am here to interview Sheriff Brown."

Not a businesswoman then, that explained the sensible flat shoes and the jacket. I should have realised earlier, it was too hot for anyone who wasn't concealing a gun to wear a jacket. Now, why would I think I recognised a State Bureau employee in South Carolina? Then she turned fully and executed a double take. Had she recognised me?

"Hi, Agent Smith …" The redhead had picked up the phone, I had half wondered about where the Secret Service Agents had gone. "An agent from SCBI, Cathy…" She struggled with her note.

"Watson, Cathy Watson." The Agent repeated. Then I connected the dots. Cathy; the mother of two and a borrowed child. Last time I had seen her she had been wearing fewer clothes. What the hell do I do now? Helen would know, except she wouldn't have recognised Agent Watson.

"Agent Smith said he will be out in a minute. Would you like me to rustle up a cup of coffee? Or, we have an order from the restaurant across the street due to be delivered, I could add it to that."

"I'll take a cup of your coffee, white, no sugar, thanks."

"Would you like a coffee too, Mr Gates? I forgot to ask when I ordered your lunch." The redhead asked, usefully giving out my name, before disappearing into the back office.

"What is your business in this office today, Mr Gates? Why are they bringing you lunch?" Cathy Watson was studying me intently.

"I came into see if I could get my car and belongings back from the Sheriff," I answered truthfully.

"So, you're the man who stirred up this mess o' beans." She was right of course, this entire tangled mess of Law Enforcement Agencies was caused by li'l' ol' me!

Agent Watson stared at me closely. "Do I know you from somewhere, Mr Gates?" That proved my point about the resort staff being invisible to the visitors.

"I believe we met on Saturday morning. Did your neighbors have a successful date weekend?"

"Ah!"

"Not that the state of your neighbors' marriage concerns me, or anybody else for that matter." I ladled as much emphasis as I could on the last few words.

"That's good to know, Mr Gates, so you'll understand why I can't say. I'll ask the Sheriff about your possessions when I get to question him."

*****

I was suddenly alone in a full building. The redhead had disappeared again, I could hear the sound of her voice but no replying sounds. I suspected she was on her phone, updating her fellow Deputies on the state of play at base.

What was the state of play? I mentally ran through how I saw it. I would need a clear picture of events for when I wrote up the story. As it would be Marlon Gates' career-defining scoop, I had to have the events clear in my mind.

Sheriff Huck Brown was somewhere in the building under arrest by the South Carolina Law Enforcement Division. Right then he was being questioned by Agent Cathy Watson of the SC Bureau of Investigation about his attempt to destroy evidence of crimes by the brother Emmett.

Emmett Brown was being held at the Federal Bureau of Investigation's pleasure for assaulting a government employee. Specifically punching Secret Service Agent Smith.

Agent Smith and his partner Agent Jones, I had to chuckle at the thought of them using false names. I am old enough to remember Alias Smith and Jones on the TV. Smith and Jones are the protection for the State's First Lady; the sister of the woman I … I what? Something, but that is not relevant right now.

The First Lady is here in her capacity as President of an anti-cruelty to animals organization, nominally to force the Sheriff to take action against his dog-kicking brother. I know there is another agenda here, do I want to reveal it?

The man from the FBI, I knew the only reason he was here was to make sure Emmett Brown faced justice for some of his actions. It would have been a gentle day out for the Fed except, I had dumped my massive conspiracy on him. He was talking about my mad meanderings with my … My what? I think I know what I want Helen to be. I am just not willing to admit it to myself, nor her until … Until what? Or do I mean when?

The front door of the Sheriff's Office building opened, setting a bell ringing. The redhead reappears behind the front desk. "Hi Bella, thanks for bringing these over."

"No problem, I have put the coffee and doughnuts for Agent Black in the box too."

"Sorry, Bella?"

"Just after you called, I got a call from this Black guy asking if I can send him over a coffee and a couple of doughnuts. I assumed it was an extra, so I put it on the Department's tab."

"Hmm, I'm not sure that the Sheriff would be —" The redhead pulled up short as a door opened and Helen and the Fed appeared.

"Is that my coffee I can smell? The order for Black?"

"Just here Agent Black, along with two doughnuts." Bella pulled a twenty-ounce cup and a paper bag out of the box.

"How much do I owe you?"

"That'll be …" Bella was trying to work out the total in her head.

"Fifteen cover it?"

"Thank you, Agent Black."

Putting his billfold back in his pocket, the Fed grabbed his purchases. "I have to make a couple of calls, but it looks like we will be checking out your theory, Mr Gates."

"Your sandwiches, Mr Gates. Compliments of the South Carolina White House." Why did I get the impression that the FBI were less than popular in Oak Lees?

I pulled the first sandwich out of the box, the hot chicken. I hand it to Helen. I noticed that she looked pale underneath her tan.

Agent Jones' head appeared around a door frame as I lifted the second giant sub out of the box. "Our Principal would like a word with you, Mr Gates, but have your lunch first."

"OK! Thanks!" I just hoped that I could get to talk to Helen properly before then. Jones responded with a thumbs-up before ducking back out of the doorway.

"I need to talk to you about Agent Jones' Principal before I meet her. Can we sit outside to eat?" Helen still looked pale and shocked. "Then you might want to share what the man from the FBI has been saying to you." I pulled the door open and followed her out into the late afternoon warmth.

*****

"How do you want me to play my encounter with the First Lady, your sister?" We had found a bench in the shade of a tree, located in the small town square." I unwrapped my sandwich, spreading the paper over my lap. "I had hoped not to meet her, that way I could have left her out of the story."

"I suppose you're going to have a field day with this." Helen was still very downbeat.

"It is going to be a huge story when the Feds start digging up bodies. If I write it, I can try to keep the story focused on the Browns and The Mob. If I don't get to do a good job, you'll end up with hundreds of hacks digging into the story looking for an angle ..."

I gestured for her to take a bite of her sandwich.

"The nudity, who you are, your folks and the rest of the family would all be game. On the other hand, whatever happens between us, I like you. I like your folks. And I like the rest of my bare-buddies at Oak Leeves too much to let that happen." I took a bite of my lunch, it was good, maybe slightly oversold. Then, nothing was going to compare with the special sandwiches I got at Alfredo's place on my rare trips to New York City. The homemade pickles made them unique.

"So, what is your plan, Theo?" I'm Theo again, I need to plan fast.

"I was thinking I have to tell the truth, just not the whole truth. Pretty much the whole thing with a few bits left out. My brush with Dog-kicker Brown and the Sheriff doing his Dukes of Hazard roleplay. Finding refuge in a Country Club, where one of the guests agrees to help me get my camera footage into safe hands. Then the bit about your Country Club being pressured to sell up. Followed by me getting the message to the FBI." I took another small bite, actually, it was quite a good sandwich. "It is the last bit I need help with. Why is the Bureau here? The real chain of events is pretty much the only way to explain it. Any thoughts?"

"I'm not sure about what exactly has happened," Helen admitted. "Agent Black has just been telling me that he needs to dig up a big chunk of the grounds, something about bodies in graves. I am so confused, I don't know what to say."

"Helen, I realise this must be a lot to take on board like this. I have been living with it all weekend, I'll try to speak to Agent Black and find out what he is planning." I started to laugh. "These Federal people have great imagination in their names; Smith and Jones. Now you tell me the FBI agent is called Black. I bet his partner is Agent White." My chuckle must have been infectious.

"Maybe it's Scarlet and their boss is White!" Helen chipped in. I went blank. "Spectrum is Green! From Captain Scarlet, the kid's TV show!"

"Sorry Helen, I must have missed that one."

"It doesn't matter. If you can find out what Agent Black is planning, I will try to keep my sister out of the way."

I chucked the last bits of bread to the birds and we headed back to the Sheriff's office.

*****

"I am aware of the sensibilities here, Mr Gates. I have been discussing arrangements with my superiors. If the Geological Physics team confirm your thoughts, we are going to need easy access to the site for anything up to four weeks. We recognise that the resort can't take that much business disruption, besides the existing roadways are too small for our needs. So ... firstly, we are going to punch a new access route through to the meadow from the road. Then we will have to fence off the probable crime scene for security. From the resort's side, it will be a privacy fence. We won't be working weekends either, there is no money for the overtime, you see." He smiled. "The space for the resort guests to enjoy will be reduced for that period. That means that there will, of course, be a payment for loss of amenity."

He screwed up the bag that his doughnuts had come in, squashed it into his coffee cup and launched the bundle into the trash can.

"Two points," I called.

"Just two? I thought that was a three-pointer." He looked at the door as if he was checking that it was closed. "Off the record, I think the new access to that meadow, where the resort wants to develop, could be worth the inconvenience. It will save them a considerable sum once building work starts. A win-win if you like."

*****

I could see they were sisters, even before Helen sat down next to her sibling. It was like looking at two peas in a pod, provided you looked beyond the difference between a hairdresser's cut 'n style and a coiffured creation and the off-the-rail dress and the couture outfit. Something, I admit I might have struggled to do a week before.

"Mr Gates, I am so pleased to meet you." Helen had warned me to expect formality and to just go with the flow. "I want to thank you personally for intervening to stop that brute from attacking a dumb animal. You took a huge risk; I saw, on the video, how he attacked you. I would have liked to thank the anonymous animal lover who passed the recording on to me too, I am the President of the League Against Animal Cruelty in this State, as part of my role as the Governor's wife. As soon as I saw the footage," she talked right through my opportunity to interject that I had been told about her Presidency. "I knew I had to act. Especially as my informant had identified the assailant as the Sheriff's brother and mentioned that you had become the subject of a manhunt for your troubles."

I went to say something, but Helen gestured I should shut up. "Thank you, Ma'am." I'm my own man, I can answer for myself. Then I have also been married twice and know it is best to just agree and shut up.

"No, once again Mr Gates, it is I who has to thank you on behalf of all mistreated animals." The First Lady leant forward, and I heard a click, as she pressed a button inside her handbag. "That is the tape off, I'll give you a copy for your story, Theo. I gather you are known as Theo at my parents' place."

"Yes, Ma'am. I think I like being Theo Galpin more than Marlon Gates, Theo seems to be a nicer person."

The First Lady laughed, and looked at her sister, mouthing something that looked like, "creeper." I'm not much of a lipreader it might have been something else.

"Thank you, Jill," Helen spoke for the first time. "Do you want to visit with Mom and Pops for a bit?"

"That would be nice, but before I do is there anything you want to ask, Theo?"

"As long as you are happy with what is on the tape, I think we have it all covered. Although I'd like to have a word with Agent Watson about getting some of my stuff back."

"I'll get that sorted, come along Bist, time for us to get changed."

*****

"… have your phone and laptop back; we arrived ahead of the Sheriff's IT guy, so they are still intact." Cathy Watson was explaining. My wallet, or what was left of it, lay on the table between us, along with my cards but no cash. My clothes: well, the crumpled, creased and soiled rags that had been my clothes, were in a used carry-out bag by my feet. The Sheriff had decided that I was a suspected drug runner too and, as such, subject to deep and personal searches. "Your car though is going to be in the shop for several days. They have dismantled it, looking for hidden substances. It is not going to be an easy rebuild either."

"Pity, it was a nice car. Still, I prefer my car being stripped and searched to having the same thing done to me."

"You are darn right there, Marlon. I don't mind the stripping but, I've seen body searches. You wouldn't like it." I wasn't sure if that was Cathy or Agent Watson talking, but whichever, she shuddered at the thought.

There was a knock at the door, Agent Smith stood outside. "When you are through, my Principal would like to have another word with you."

"I think we are finished here, aren't we, Agent Watson?"

"If there is anything else, I know where to find you." Her smile hid our shared secret.

*****

"Where is your colleague, Agent Jones hiding out?" I asked Smith as he guided me, not that I was sincerely interested in the movements of the Secret Service. I was, however, interested in how much they knew about their Principal's family. Were they in on the secret?

"Jones has just driven your friend back to the resort, she had to collect something for the First Lady. Here we are, in here." It was the door to the Sheriff's private office. It appeared that the answer I had been probing for was 'not a lot!' The Agent knocked and pushed the door open for me to enter. He didn't follow, pulling it shut behind me.

"How did it go, Theo?"

"I am pleased to say I am going to be staying in these parts a while longer, my car is in pieces."

"You're sure you are pleased?"

"Yep!"

"Don't you have a story to write? Copy to submit or whatever it is journalists do?"

"I've gotten my laptop back. So, now I can write up my story, and maybe the next, anywhere." I love technology when it works for me!

"Isn't there someone queuing to become your next wife?"

"Next wife?" In my guise of Marlon Gates might have been divorced twice. "In the North? Certainly not for this Galpin! However, I have hopes that a certain Carolina lady —" I was pretty certain that the woman who kissed me enthusiastically on the lips wasn't the *First* Lady of South Carolina. Although, Theo had been celibate until a few days earlier. So in one way, Helen was my first lady. Happy, silly thoughts filled my head. Our kiss finally came to an end. I stepped back slightly so that I could look into her eyes. "Helen, I don't have anything to hurry back north for." That was true, "I don't even have a pet of any sort!" Let alone a dog, I added thinking back to events of the previous week. "And I love you."

"Theo, I was so scared. It has been a long time since someone said those three little words to me and meant it. I …" She took a deep breath and changed the direction of our conversation. "Please forgive me for behaving like a silly adolescent." I could tell there was a lot of old pain underlying that evasive swerve.

Ted Bun

Chapter 10

The cup of coffee by my side of the bed was barely tepid. The early morning sunlight slanting through the curtains had lost its orange hint as it moved from illuminating the walls across the floor. "I have a couple of questions. If I meet your sister again, what do I call her?"

"It is not a case of if, it is a when; unless you've changed your mind?"

"Nope, I'm hoping to become a fixture." I had plans to enable this relocation.

"In which case, call her Jill."

"The politics?"

"The politics will take care of themselves. What was your other question?"

"Well, I know the answer I want to this question, what would you like me to call you, for now? Your real name, Helen or something else? 'Bis' was it Jill called you?"

That made her laugh, "Not 'Bist' that would be inappropriate! Keep calling me Helen, please, Theo!" That was good to hear! "I've been Helen for so long now, it is what I am known by almost everybody. Besides, I chose the name for myself, I'd read a version of the Greek myths and fancied myself held in a walled city."

"And why is 'Bist' inappropriate?" Journalist, I ask questions to get at the story behind the words.

"My sister, I was always her 'Big Sister' but she struggled as a baby and I became her 'Bist' and between the two of us, it stuck." Another piece of family history fell into place.

"That is nice. My brother used to call me 'Rat', he said it was short for 'Brat'."

I miss him. He was killed in the Twin Towers attack, one of the over three hundred firefighters who died that day. That is something that can wait until later before I share it but share it I must. Helen will need to understand why I get very low for a couple of days around the 9-11 anniversary.

It would be nice to understand what caused the pain that Helen still felt. I hope that time will build the trust needed for her to revisit that hurt, or at least allow it to heal.

A kiss interrupted my thoughts.

"Cummon Brat! We need to get up, the Feds will be here with their gear in an hour." Helen leapt out of bed, pulling the sheet off me.

"What's the rush, Bist? It is not as if we have to get dressed!" I chased her to the bathroom, laughing.

*****

When the FBI Geo-physics team arrived, we were dressed. Well sort of. I had a towel wrapped around my waist, gym style, as I led the two large trucks with their trailers up to the meadow. Helen, swathed in a light sarong, was briefing the team leader on the local ground rules. I gathered afterwards it was a case of: "Don't stare at naked people. Don't make personal comments. Don't take photographs. And if you want to use the pool, do so nude." Oh, and she will have mentioned towels.

The first trailer was a mobile home turned into a computer suite. The other was a generator to power their gear. The boxes and bags that filled the truck beds contained the tools of their trade. I stayed to watch, journalistic curiosity, but I left after an hour. It was less exciting than watching the guys painting white lines down the freeway. Their gear looked sort of similar, wheels, a box in the middle and a handle to steer it with.

They walked up and down the meadow all day long. Then the following day they pushed their equipment from side to side, putting small flags into the ground as they went. "Markers, where we reckon there is a significant change in the sub-soil structure.

The leader told me, as we shared a couple of beers beside the pool.

"How many locations have you marked?" I was going to say graves, but at the moment there was no proof they were graves rather than some other ground anomaly.

"Fourteen, and we still have a couple of sweeps to finish. If you pressed me I'd say twenty or twenty-one similar anomalies" That was where I had picked up the word, I realised.

Chapter 11

The bulldozers started putting in the new access on the following Monday morning. The ground penetrating radar had identified some twenty potential graves. I can call them graves now since a quick investigative trench across one site found human bones. At least it wasn't Labour Day for weeks. Mondays were quiet. I started work on my story. The copy for the fraud case had been submitted to various editors. I had been assured that I would get a by-line and payment when it came to court. Small beer compared to the story being unearthed in front of my eyes.

The FBI had brought in several teams of scientists and technicians, a tent was put up over the grave, they were all graves as far as I was concerned. Over the weeks, the teams dug, scraped, sifted and sieved their way through the twenty-one sites marked by the Geo-physicists recovering a skeleton from each, along with various artefacts, jewellery, watches, plastic cards, coins, buttons and bullets. Thousands of photographs of the location were taken as more articles were uncovered. Eventually, the human remains were stretchered away into Coroner's Office vehicles. The personal items were bagged up to help with the eventual identification of the deceased. The bullets, which had been recovered from almost every grave, were sent away to labs across the country for forensic analysis in an effort to match them to the gun from which they were fired.

I got to chat with a member of the Coroner's team, he confirmed what I had hoped. The state of decomposition of the bodies, they were all little more than skeletons, meant that they were more than ten years in the ground. They had been interred before Oak Leeves was established.

My contact in the SCBI, Cathy, and her family had visited a couple more times during the investigation. They were on the waiting list for membership of the resort.

Cathy had suggested a few names of people who worked at the Coroner's who may have talked to the press in the past. That was how I got to read all the summaries of the Pathologist's reports.

The bodies, including some women, were so far decomposed that evidence of soft tissue injuries had all been lost. However, all the skeletons showed major injuries. Bullet wounds mainly, some had multiple fractures, showing they had been violently beaten before dying of their injuries or a bullet, normally delivered to the skull.

One body caused a certain amount of confusion. The initial, in situ post-mortem examination, revealed nothing obvious in the way of wounds or cause of death. It was several weeks before the Medical Examiner came through with a conclusion. I got to see a full copy of his report. Don't ask, a secret shared and all that.

Jane Doe #4, was female. A small adult, less than five feet tall, light build, possibly Asian. That the ME found only minor joint damage or wear suggested her age at death was in the range between her mid-twenties and early thirties. He detected no post-gravida changes or other evidence of childbirth. What he had found on examination, was a fractured hyoid bone, indicative of manual strangulation.

The Medical Examiner had postulated, that she had been a prostitute, probably strangled in a sex game gone too far.

If she was lucky, Jane Doe would be reunited with her name via dental records or DNA. The only means of identification available to her and all the bodies but one.

Herman Brown, aka Pa Brown, had been buried with a pistol. The gun was identified as his personal Saturday night special. It was found positioned between his thigh bones. There was a lot of damage to his lower spine, suggesting a particularly nasty and humiliating form of execution.

*****

Shortly after the discovery of Pa Brown's remains, Emmet Brown turned State's evidence and disappeared into the Federal Witness Protection Program. The arrests started soon after.

While I was chasing around like an idiot, trying to get quotable quotes from people involved in uncovering the 'Mobs Graveyard' as it became known, the Fraud case that had brought me to Oak Lees slowly went belly up. Such is the life of a Freelance Journalist.

On the positive side, Marlon had finally gotten his big story. It got syndicated coast to coast. It was his big payday. He even published the story as a book. It sold well and made the best-seller lists in the Sunday papers. In the end, though, there was no peace in it for him. Anonymous threats were made. No horse's heads were delivered to his Jersey City apartment. Instead, it got firebombed. He wasn't home. He hasn't filed a story or been seen in any of his old haunts since.

His once blue Dodge Charger was found burnt out in the desert, a dozen miles outside of Las Vegas, a month after his home was torched. The search that followed failed to find a body or any clue as to how the car got to its final resting place or what had happened to the driver.

His ex-wife published a kiss and tell, "The Journalist Who Vanished", which sought to trace his last few weeks. It gave details of e-mails and phone calls from Las Vegas, where he "had been talking to his source about another scoop."

Some people thought it wasn't written in her voice and the book had been ghostwritten. They were technically correct, Marlon Gates was a ghost. I had decided to quit journalism and Marlon was no more. All that remained of his journalistic career was a byline in archived copies of old newspapers. Of the man, nothing.

Theo Galpin's forged documents were replaced by genuine cards, permits and licenses. Thanks to the support of the South Carolina Bureau of Investigation. Agent Watson, Cathy, as I called my liaison, had managed to maneuver me onto the Witness Protection Scheme, I was a witness in the misuse of public office case against Huck Brown and my life had been in danger.

Cathy and I had put together a report to the SCBI, in which we pointed out that there were numerous places where domestic terrorists could gather and plot violent acts, unobserved by security agencies. Places where Government Agents are excluded through fear of losing their job. We cited a case in France, where it took over a year, and a holidaying British Bobby to crack a money laundering gang.

Cathy has secretly been appointed as the first Special Agent (N). It is a pilot. So far, she hasn't detected anything untoward, but then she has yet to access every naturist space in South Carolina.

I had already discovered that I enjoyed talking to people without an agenda influencing everything I said.

*****

Now, a year later, I spend my days welcoming people to Oak Leeves and project managing the building of the new pool and hotel on the site. It sounds complicated but it is a case of making sure the contractors are keeping to schedule and not over-ordering materials.

I have met Jill several times, and her husband, Franklin twice. Yes, I call the Governor by his first name. "I have to get used to it; I have decided to get out of politics. I want to be out from under the media spotlight. The kids want to be able to come and swim in Grandmom's pool and hear Grandpop's stories of holidays in France." He was nearing the end of his second term in the State House. It is probably for the best.

Helen and I plan to announce our wedding date at the first full family Christmas in fifteen years. Jill is very excited about being her Sister's Matron of Honor. She has been a regular visitor as she and Helen plan and prepare for her big day. Jill has given up the strict secrecy that used to surround her visits. She still has her security detail. Agent Smith sits outside the gates to the resort, watching people coming and going from the car. Agent Jones does close protection from her sun bed by the pool. She has a nice all-over tan; it was at her suggestion that we are putting in an outdoor gym.

Some evenings, I get to sit quietly in a corner, fetching refreshments as required while Helen and Jill spend hours talking about catering arrangements, guest lists and dresses - if any. One time, as I carried a tray in from the kitchen I caught the tail end of a conversation, Jill was talking, "… first time I met him I told you he was a 'keeper'!"

I spend my spare time working on my second work of fiction, The Journalist Who Vanished" had been such a success.

"Besides," Franklin had confided, while we were sharing war stories over a beer one afternoon. "Having a whole family of naturists, wife, children and in-laws, would not have gone down well with the more conservative voters. If it had got out they might have started …" His frosted beer glass slipped through his fingers. "Oops, another pair of trousers ruined …"

"Not!" We finished in unison.

Ted Bun

Other Books by Ted Bun
The Rags to Riches Novellas

The Uncovered Policeman
The Uncovered Policeman Abroad
The Uncovered Policeman: In and Out of the Blues
The Uncovered Policeman: Goodbye Blues
Two Weddings and a Naming
The Uncovered Policeman: Caribbean Blues
The Uncovered Policeman: Family Album
A Spring Break at L'Abeille Nue
The Uncovered Policeman: Made for TV
The Uncovered Policeman: The Long Road
The Uncovered Policeman: Live, Laugh and Love
The Uncovered Policeman: A New Home in the Sun
While Bees Sleep

Rags to Riches Short Stories

The Cutters' Tale
The Naked Warriors
The Girls Trip to the Beach
Cocoa and Pyjamas
Forty Shades of Green
BareAid
The Uncovered Policeman's Casebooks
The Bridesmaid's Tale

Other Novellas

New House … New Neighbours
New House … New Address
New House … New Traditions

The Summer of '71 (A Crooke and Loch story)

Runners and Riders (A Crooke and Loch story)
The Summer of '76 (A Crooke and Loch story)
A Line of Death (A Crooke and Loch story)

Problems and Passions (NBL Solutions 1)
Problems of Succession (NBL Solutions 2)
Problems in the Pyrenees (NBL Solutions 3)

When the Music Stops: DC al Fine (MFL 1)
Then Play On (MFL 2)
24 Bar Rest (MFL 3)

Paul Mount is Special Squirrel
The Day Before Last
Frozen Assets
The Madison Interview

After The Event
The Last Day of June

Other Short Stories
Going South – Forever
The Dancer
A Job in the City
New Laws
Melissa, More or Less

About Ted Bun

I was born in London and have lived most of my life in the south of England. I only include that fact to explain the Lundin Axcint I write in.

I had what could be called a portfolio career. However, the diversity of experience is starting to pay off now.

After a lifetime of not knowing what to do, I decided to do something new. I announced I was retiring and Mrs Bun agreed. We spent two years searching before we found L'Olivette, our little paradise in the South of France, and started offering relaxing holidays in our gîte.

During the long evenings of the quiet season, a novella started to take shape, "The Uncovered Policeman." A light, cosy mystery romance with a cast of pleasant happy people, with quirky characters. It was first published on Valentine's Day 2016.

The characters wrote themselves into a series of twelve books, with short stories and other books set in the same world.

Other people had come along and whispered their stories in my ear, as I tried to sleep by the pool. So, I wrote their tales down too, hence the number of books listed above.

Follow my blog at – www.tvhost.co.uk

Printed in Great Britain
by Amazon